Fiction

I0666751

Lit for Nothin

By

LES COOK

Travel Intrigue

Lit for Nothin:

First edition. Published 2019

Contact: Les Cook

Lescook360@gmail.com

Library and Archives Canada

Printed book ISBN 978-1-9990023-0-5

Electronic book ISBN 978-1-9990023-1-2

Context

Chapter 1...

Chapter 2...

Chapter 3...

Screws

Chapter 4...

Dynamic Affect

Lotus Affect

Chapter 5...

Chapter 6...

Chapter 7...

Ivory

Chapter 8...

Chapter 9...

———

Amazon Peru

Spirited Drink

Chapter 10...

Chapter 11...

Live in a Tree – Hide in a Cave

Chapter 12...

Honey - Home

Chapter 13...

Chapter 14...

Chapter 15...

The Case

1

Look at Arthur Rimbaud at eighteen.

I'm fifty

Give me food, shelter, a walkway to a train, boat, and a house of ill repute.

I want everything on the first page

—

END THIS PERFECT LIFE now so I can begin.

She looked at me and said, 'You are that used to death, that you can say it so calm like that?'

I'm not used to death – I'm used to hearing it . . . that is all.

I made a decision eighteen months ago, as I stood at my open bedroom door looking past my wife to the empty hall – it wasn't a specific thing I was going to change; it was going to be a sale.

A tunnel of hell blew through my mind soul universe – the sound barrier burst my ears to a slight non-painful tinge as I travelled near the speed of light until quiet, alone, dark, and hollow.

No longer travelling forwards or backwards.

When you travel this fast, you stop moving, find harmony.

I knew it would be more than a few months of heartache to reach peace.

'Hell' some would say.... I don't believe in 'Hell' – I'll come out the other-side.

Cell of horror – let us be real, it is minor compared to what some feel – this is education, not competition.

The deal made the decision conceived is mine alone – one man, one secret – can't tell a soul otherwise someone, something will know and my reward will fail.

Is it my fault family members are passing away?

The second to die was my Father – four of his brothers in a row, in twelve months eight relatives gone – this is domino... the last my nephew.

Seven die in ill health.

The eighth in the spell my nephew – except he ended the curse, he's missing – yes bothersome.

Missing is a gift – he politely stopped and spat on the spell – the curse in limbo as he cannot be found.

Human – blame the spirits if you have nowhere else to turn.

Am I so naive that I believe I have this ability – this influence to be scorned harmful energy?

It has been months since the Boy, my nephew, went missing in the river, they say.

My twenty-year-old nephew will always be the Boy.

To visit my sister and my brother-in-law was – I have no words, no short story, no poem, no earthling can articulate feelings I held.... I could not speak, I could not cry – disbelieve and why.

Tragedy.

I've said my peace, nothing more to tell – none of us know what happened. We've all been intercepted. The Boy is gone he has not been found.

Death by misadventure, if you are to die young, misadventure is a choice one could make.

You see... you've come into the story at the wrong time.

You will listen to the results.

I, the flawed, must live.

I should be in a shack I don't own – no job, just fun.

It isn't like this, I have two homes – I want nothing.

My Machine head says don't invest in sugar, sorrow, crooks, or charity after the fact.

I call reasoning 'Machine' to fit into the modern scheme of intelligence.

My wife says I'm smart – 'Smart for nothing'. A smart that is useless in the real world. I like it; I have no desire to be a function screw in the world built.

She can summon fire, surround me in flames, cool me in the sea.

Her and mine equal love and hate in this marriage.

'Why aren't you naked?' my wife asks. Don't you have to be naked when you get a massage?' she laughs.

No, not naked.

'Come on, take off your clothing – just leave your underwear on.'

Pale, what am I to do once I liked to be pale – before I didn't like pale skin – things change.

A tune up, is this what she is getting at.

Doesn't matter, my wife arranged and will pay the masseuse.

Everything that you expect a saint to be my wife is not – than again she is not Christian – she is no angel – she is not perfect – she is beyond what perfect should be – my Buddha, my teacher, my spiritual test. Her hair shines, her smile smirks away slight dishonesty – oh, but if you are on her side – the wicked is good, the lies funny, and the sly cool.

I don't care enough to lie; lie is to save yourself – I care enough to tell the truth; truth is hope to save oneself.

I have my faults – ruined any greatness early in my life – cannot undo the wrongs I've thought.

Diabolical – criminal – am I sick?

No, I'm incapable of sensibility. I believe in the unreal – the mind moves matter routine.

Labels are flexible, all parts of the human condition are in us – it is the attached label you must watch out for.

My wife tells the masseuse to stop.

The tune up is over.

I roll over to my stomach. She pays the masseuse – escorts her to the door.

We make love, installing memory to our skin that our minds absorb – goodbye children.

I'll miss this Cambodian puzzle

I'm going to Canada, Lake Wapa, British Columbia. The place I grew up.

My wife, relaxed and showered, is on the phone – speaking to her friends she loans money to, the collateral she's to keep, the payments she's to collect, six-month plans – two-week plans – business opportunities, she swears, talks loud – then calm. She laughs when she hears the answers she likes – she'll send our fourteen-year-old son to collect interest payments – or perhaps earnings from arrangements – she lends at a better rate than the bank. I don't listen – I won't see the money or lose the money I leave it to her . . .

I'm thinking of my flight to Canada, and how I'll neglect or fix my $120,000 debt.

Revolving earth.

Years ago, I was in Sri Lanka, swimming, writing, on my way to India. A friend owed me a minor debt – Cambodia I went instead of India to collect the debt.

I never thought wife – I thought visit friend, collect debt, and wonder at Khmer Temple Architecture.

I never did collect the debt – met my wife instead.

My wife says throw the thought of lost money away, if it wasn't for your friend we would have never met – sometimes the result of loss takes on a different form.

I have no strength to go to work – I have no plans to go to work, they've called and I've not answered, I have answered see you in the spring.

I have poetry and theory to attend.

I feel I still have jealousy – I still have how will I make money – I still have is my family safe – I still have should I continue to waste time and write or should I be working every minute of my life?

Should I have an affair?

If you do not live, what kind of poetry will it be? I want to go live in the trees find truth – or is it better to find truth in the city social every day? Both I say, to capture answers sought. Live it and reflect upon it.

Bank it.

What I know about death is nothing – I've never seen it – my wife has seen death, killing, massacre, covered the awful smell of death decay with clay.

She has a look of someone I've never met – a look that tells me she's been killed, lived, and will not be killed again.

A real story would be about her, not me.

She once told me, 'When you eat ants, they bite your tongue.'

How can I argue with that?

I'm not ready to face my story with her.

I'm facing alcohol today, jetlag and coffee tomorrow.

Mostly I'm to face family and friends – Christmas is near.

Jetlag

Jetlag – the zombie, how can you complain? Stay awake and wake up, that's all you have to do.

Every time I fly back to Canada I say never again – jetlag kills – if in my mind or real. Doesn't matter.

They say flying west to Asia from North America is easier then flying east from Asia to North America. I think that's true.

My answer to jetlag = endure.

No coffee. No alcohol. A fifteen-hour time change four days in sponsoring myself, I'm okay.

I've quit drinking many times, for months, for weeks, days, hours, and once for a decade. I realize all the tricks and I'm ready for them this time.

Had a relapse. Drank tequila, drank two coffees. No problem, start counting today.

I'm an expert at quitting and pretty good at starting too.

The liquor drink is long gone as a threat.... it is friend to establishment and an enemy to the people.

What is passé?

If celebrated they've already had their best day.

Coffee – I don't know what to do about that. It is unfortunate that things get started on coffee. I'm drinking it now as I attempt to write about Spirited Drink (Alcohol). Maybe I can't add to the subpar that an intoxicated genius can.

My name is 'Fortune' L Ce Fortune.

2

LAKE WAPA, BRITISH Columbia – alone.... not so alone, I have my mother, sister, relatives, a few friends.

Yes, I'm more alone than I've ever been.

Bohemian.

I'm back, walking along the lake.

There are no stunt scenes in this story.

The lakes are beautiful, but I've been on them before and now I don't care.

Valley lakes are warm enough to swim in the summer, ice in the winter.

Now winter, the ice has begun.

No hash, no cocaine. Opium? I'm writing instead. Write, solving problems instead of committing crime, smashing the system with words instead of aggression.

Drink – if you give me only one drink – please give me a brick I can throw through the liqueur cabinet window too.

Sure, I'm happy, because I have my mind.

I'm a romantic. If I was rich I'd write, and poor, you know I've made myself poor, the romantic the sexy the cool thing to do.

Write. You'll be rich. You'll be poor.

Lake Wapa is many and nothing – a lake resort, a mountain resort. Camping, fishing, hiking, hunting, eco tourism... snow sports, water sports. Which direction will you go today?

Lake Wapa would be a city if you gathered it all together. It isn't a city though – it only acts utilizing all of them.

I utilize none of them – I'm broke. I can walk along the lake, sprint the forest trails.

I throw wonder wall out of the window.

Beethoven for the day.

Da Clash Dub rock.

Rimbaud – 'A Season in Hell'.

Listen to The Stones every day.

Lit... for nothing is no joke.

'Do you want to speak to Tru?' my Mother asks.

My heart stops, my mind abuzz.

Tru is a long-time friend – dangerous, provocative.

Tru does things I don't aspire to – he's fun. The amazing thing – he gets me – and I take the good over the bad from him.

Four parts: human, animal, machine, unknown.

You can call them gods (that is a joke).

If I don't have ears, if I don't have eyes, what does the outer world mean to me? It is hard not to look to the outside surrounding world when flying on a jet plane.

I say how ancient, how silly, how ~~fucking~~ noisy!

Am I now writing my last book, as this is an ancient way of learning, of entertaining, of communicating?

So when I picked up the phone I say, 'Yes. I'll stop by tomorrow or the next day.' Tru says he'll pick me up, drop me off if I don't have transportation. I have transportation; my mother's new vehicle.

Everyone talked about his game – because he talked about his game, though he doesn't give up details.

(Tru) The brute and I best friends – how did that happen?

I've turned fifty years old – he's fifty-three. What a life.

Tru is naturally strong – thick, not tall at all. He has striking facial features, gray-brown wavy hair. Looks mean, used to dress in exercise gear or jeans. How he looks, acts, what he wears now, I don't know. Mostly the same I suppose, nothing changes every five years I see him.

He once made a child, except the woman ran away to the Eastern part of Canada. He says he'll never have a child again.

Tru has a way of finding things out and not just because he has a wide circle of friends who tell him information for favors owed or favors needed. Tru is in touch. He has built the seen and unseen Internet. He knew I was around.

He owns three homes on the same street – two of his best friends also own homes there. It is an insolated road of thirty properties, with an alley in the middle as the road circles around the two rows of houses. Behind is a mountain park, in front is a sparse forest and highway before the shore of the lake. His personal fortress with good neighbors on both sides – he's been laying favors for most in the neighborhood, and the others ignore him. There is a reason he's stayed on this road for over twenty-five years.

His home is a 1980's two-bedroom bungalow – the wooden siding needs replacing – a wire-mesh fence surrounding the yard. His other homes are bigger, better, well kept, and maybe that's the point.

When I reach the wire-mesh fenced entrance his dog begins to bark – it is a different dog than I remember but it is the same set up, a variation of a bulldog. I walk around to the back yard as there is a path between his home and his neighbor. Tru is already at the back door inviting me in so I enter the kitchen.

A beautiful woman who must be forty – demented to the core – is leaning against the counter, Tru asks her to suck my ~~cock~~. She's already sipping beer, I don't drink. I think he's joking and I don't oblige, I don't say, 'Here is my ~~cock,~~' I'm naturally stoned it doesn't matter.

She is attractive as ~~fuck~~ in all the wrong ways; you couldn't love her, she's corrupted.

'She's to marry tomorrow. Don't worry about it,' he says to me.

'Right?' he says to her.

'Yes I'm getting married tomorrow.' She moves towards me.

A desire I fear as she comes near before passing me for a cigarette outside. She's lucky it is a warm winter day with no chance of snow or rain. Tru hasn't changed; he still hates the sight and smell of cigarette smoke.

Tru pulls me aside. 'I ~~fucked~~ her this morning. She'll ~~suck~~ you off if you want. She likes you, she said so. Do you remember her?'

I remember her... she was the best looking nineteen-year old that never left town. I knew her older sister well.

I don't answer Tru. He accepts I can't or won't unless pressed. Not long after she finishes her cigarette she orders a taxi and leaves.

Tru, in classic voice: 'She's getting old now.'

'She's still lovely.'

'I know, if you want to find a younger woman forget it – they only want money, that's it. I have another girl, beautiful just like her, except young, twenty-six years old. I'm putting her through college. If I didn't pay for her degree – buy her clothes – she wouldn't come around. She'd find another man to take care of her. That's it man – money. They may fall in love, but it isn't like it was when we were young. They aren't shy. They say money first, love second, and it isn't even love, it is an agreement to have sex.'

'Sometimes they fall in love.'

'Sure, you're right, but they hold it against you. "I love you, so you have to pay me because I love you." You have to pay them because they've fallen in love with you. Like it's your fault.'

Tru tries to be good. He thinks I'm good... to a limit. . . at least he tries to be 50% good.

'What do you do over there in Cambodia?' is always a question and Tru is no different.

'Swimming, hiking, reading, drinking, dancing – I'm writing a book.'

These aren't the answers they want – they want to know about money.

'Do you work over there?' he asks.

Micro-financing, I say, in business with my wife.

'You loan money.' He is stunned.

Small amounts – she collects a few hundred on interest a month. My wife calls it karma lending. Sometimes you lose the money but are rewarded in karma. It is a small income she can afford and I can invest – she makes more than I do.

'That's okay, how much money do you need over there?'

More than that, I have to come back to Canada to make real money.

I'm not successful at money ventures. Tru claims to be – but really in the end game maybe I'm the one who has success. I loan money to remain outstanding in the community. He loans money in the community for financial gain...the feel of power. Loaning money that isn't yours is the best policy – just ask the bank.

'You still working Safety in the oil fields?' he asks.

Every year, I answer, living at camp or a hotel.

That's where my income comes, Safety Advisor to oilrigs, gas plants, and construction sites. Where else can I make money where they feed, shelter, transport? And I can't hurt myself, no risk to life . . . nothing. My expenses are nothing – except when I come visit friends like him. This is why I stopped. Some would say I could make more money if I visited friends like him.

Tru no longer has a muscle car – he has a compact four-door pickup truck. Is the dirt bike gone too? Nope, the bike is in the garage with the snow mobile.

Tru does what most of us think and talk but don't do – he's still in shape. He has to be.

We walk to the park behind his home in the forest mountainside and talk, leaving his dog behind. He says he'll take his dog out for a jog later, on a different trail.

The snow is near melted on the well-used hard packed gravel trail.

'There are other ways to make money,' Tru says. 'I know you aren't working now.'

'I'm supposed to return to work in the spring,' I answer.

'That's a long time.'

'I have things I'm doing.'

'You need money. You know the deal.'

I know the consequences working for him – a black eye, a sore jaw, possible loss of funds, possible windfall of funds, possibly need a lawyer. Happy-free-sad-in ruin. Still, all these aren't the reasons the reasons I may refuse. I promised myself I'd not enter this kind of life. Learn from it, stay on the hinges – entertainment.

'You don't have to borrow money. We have other ways. Work together.'

'How much can I make in six months?'

'Six months will just get you started.'

'Eight months?'

'Nine is better.' Tru is firm.

Take your gun and aim at me as we are essentially enemies in the human sense, but yes, enemies understand each other, can love each other. When Tru points a gun when I'm late on a loan he will think rationally and not in material investment, but emotional investment.

'So what have you learnt over there?' He asks of my overseas adventure.

I didn't necessarily learn over there, it just gives me the time to document and expand upon it.

I learned where we are going.

'Where are we going?' He asks.

'I've learned we are going backwards in time.'

'How so?'

'To capture it in one sentence – maybe I can't say correctly at this time – it might not be what you think.'

'Take your time. I want to hear this. When you talk, I listen.'

'I will say our technology is ancient ...and everything we've begun to invent and create is already inside us.'

A medium sized dog runs towards us, barking aggressively. A tall, middle aged man wearing a thin downfield jacket and blue jeans is walking behind the dog smiling like a tit, as his dog doesn't know if it should protect him, or greet us. 'Don't worry he's just friendly,' the man says.

Tru doesn't give the dog a chance to get close – he takes a stone out of his pocket and throws it at the dog, intentionally missing its head, then he grabs a fallen tree branch – in case the ragged shepherd doesn't heel but the shepherd holds steady barking.

Tru addresses the dog's owner. 'If you don't tell that dog to stop barking, I will.'

The man responds: 'He's just friendly – you are freighting the poor animal'

'He's aggressive. Call him off.' Tru consults the man.

The owner whistles – his dog disobeys, backing and barking as we walk closer.

The owner quickly run's up and takes the dog's collar in his hand, holds the dog to the side of the trail as we pass.

'Where's your leash?' Tru asks.

The man mumbles, swears.

Tru turns and confronts the man. 'That shepherd jumped up on my neighbor the other day – dirtying her clothes – you want to pay for the dry cleaning? Next time use a leash.'

Tru has done what I'd like to do – a German shepherd police dog bit me when I was thirteen years old as I was coming out of the woods on a trail leading down a hill to my home. I wasn't breaking any law – the police constable was off duty behind the leash-less dog. He didn't say anything, just stared dumbfounded – no apology, nothing. I don't even think he called his dog. The constable lived across the street from us. I can't say he liked me or us. He wasn't into communication. He was into being a dick. I complained to my mother but she said nothing until weeks later when my sister was bit by the same German shepherd. My mother said something then.

After this incident I knew not all policemen were your friends – he was Royal Canadian Mountie. I'm not going to begin bashing Mounties – many have been good to me – when a police man is good you say they are a good human being – when police disrespect you, you put the police in one large dumping pot. It should be the other way around, one bad cop and the rest role model.

We continue on our way.

Tru looks at me, and laughs. 'I let my dog run without a leash on the other side of the hill – nobody walks over there as it's too far and if they do they are usually so scared that they don't say ~~fuck~~. But this guy he doesn't apologize, nothing, so I give him a hard time. Besides, he's lucky I could let my dog loose and my boy would chew his dog to pieces. But I'm a nice guy. He doesn't even say thank you when I plow the snow along the road in front of his home. I plow the entire street and alley for everyone in my neighborhood.'

I have the thoughts, I haven't the fury, but every once in a while, I do. Tru knows this. He expects more if it from me and I expect less of it from him. He does things I'd think about doing or my aggressive self threatens but I stall, I complain, instead of doing – perhaps I write.

Tru checks his smart phone. 'I just want to let you know that when we get back to the house the young woman that I'm putting through college that I told you about this morning, she'll be at the house. I think you will like her; she is a good girl, she just wants to have fun, that is all. You'll enjoy talking to her – I want her to keep coming around. If you stay and visit it would show a different side of me. Stick around for a little bit. I'll order in lunch. Talk to her like you talk to me. I don't want to fuck her today... so have lunch.'

It has always been like this – we are extreme opposites that get along for the journey of knowledge. Many can learn from another but they can't stand the minutes together – as to say information is free if you can stand the company that gives it.

The young woman he is putting through college is mildly attractive. She's ticked at Tru, I'm the buffer... soon lunch is over and she's gone back to school. A friend once told me that women like Tru because he's good at sex. Depending on the woman I guess.

I'm invited back next week.

He will ask me again to come work with him, I'm sure.

My mother, my sister, my brother-in-law, all my relatives, all my friends ask me about work...when will I be going back to work? And none of them understand – I can't – I can't perform the same theater play for ten years. I'm a great actor, but even the great actors become stale boring in the same role until it is the only role they play.

Before at work it was simple.

Now I have past the strike – real or imaginary, all the gains I've made gone. A pattern occurs – I began to cheat a little, warping my person, no longer able to do the job well. Hidden weaknesses have come forth, no longer able to rely on the invisible to help me out.

I want this performance to end now before I'm labeled.

3

THE YEAR BEFORE LAST I kinda stopped drinking and I'd started to gamble, specifically on sports betting because I didn't drink when I gambled.

This was it, the missing puzzle . . . sports betting could be my alternative to drinking – super.

This is going to be great. Not only will I not be drinking as much. I can also make the money that I would have drunk.

So it began.

And it was working. I was drinking very little.

Betting was expensive – though worth it compared to the cost of my wellbeing, or lack of it from drinking.

Soon though . . .

I'd drink when I lost – and then I'd drink when I won – and finally I drank while I gambled – experiment over.

It's funny, Charles Bukowski the poet, a notorious alcoholic had to stop drinking, Doctors orders and he's like, "What will I do now?" – and his I think girlfriend said, "Go to the horse track. You can bet on them."

Dumbstruck, he was like, "They bet on horses to see who will win?"

And she gives him details.

So he went to the track, gambled, and that was it – he was hooked – loved it – and experienced a surge in his Poetry when he returned from the track.

If he didn't go to the track he couldn't write.

He never did stop drinking.

So I sit, no drinking, no gambling.

Now what?

—

Walking through my Ruins.

Hometown – no fever no long-lost love, there is always some but nothing to fight for, nothing to bamboozle.

I'm stranded.

The most interesting story I can't tell:

'You write like a hieratic,' my award-winning author friend told me.

There is no ghost – there is only your mind and what you produce.

The hungry ghost is you.

Ghosts are real; your truth, your fears.

Spirit – ever changing, like our being.

Have your God – the smallest object in the universe or the largest object in the universe, it doesn't matter – alone it is nothing. No God – just an object you focus on.

If you try to explain Ghost or God you will become confused. If you say it in one sentence or think of it in simple terms you will understand.

A feeling is a feeling. It doesn't have to be explained – it can be understood quickly with little thought.

When you argue, over think it, over-write it, is when the competing parts come into play. Competing parts nullify an answer and you are left with others telling you the answer for God, Gods, and Ghost.

Your choice is that of your soul-mind-body being.

You are many... Gods are many.

Lone – is nothing without another.

If you say something has to start from something than you have a God – it is nothing alone until it creates something else and so on and so on.

You yourself have its own God – The Gods of many of everything that you are. Some of these parts create ghosts – others create miracles, guardians, monsters, serenity, and misery.

What parts of you travel I can't say.

The so-called heaven and so-called hell –

Buddha kind of got it – but others change it for better or worse

Buddha is a vehicle to a wider world.

Take them all, take what you like, but like everything they are never made as one – they are made up of many.

If I dare say Gods not God if the divine theory is what you worship.

I wanted to slap her first, assault her verbally until she cried and begged me to come to her – that is how we met and ultimately how we finished.

Except I didn't slap her. I verbally scolded her, told her she needed me as a lover, quit hiding, tell the truth, seek your desire – and after a month of hints where at times she cried, swore, made attempts to strike, she came to me and I seduced her without her crying, swearing, or striking.

Her name is Veronica, she's beyond forty years old, an only child brought up by her grandparents. Her parents died when she was young.

She's just entered my mother's living room.

She would have been good at law enforcement. As I was told I would have been good at breaking the law.

She did run off, thought she was going to be a Royal Canadian Mounted Police Officer – I took it personally, like she was going to find me, arrest me, or marry me. I could go completely clean – it wouldn't have been a problem. She phoned and I never showed to greet her – end of story, no, our original story reignited as friendship, the common man's mistake, but in this case, it was the correct choice. She never did become a police officer; she opened a security service with the money from her parent's estate.

Veronica is always my argument – she'll revert back to the original absolute impossible but when the winds came together and the fire burned it was heaven with her, so peaceful, so quiet and tight. Not many I could hold for hours – she was one – she was worth a summer of storms for the calm of one night in autumn, maybe three evenings if I didn't speak. We still have not ~~fucked~~ as animals. The strength is still here.

We are alone for the first time in years.

She asks me, 'What do you do now?'

Swim, go for walks, read.

'For a living,' she corrects me.

'I'm not working.'

'What do you do?' – is a stupid question I think to myself. How about, 'Who are you?' Who are you is a good start.

I like hiking and dancing. I've been receiving money from working in Environmental Health and Safety in the gas and oil industry.

I haven't even mentioned writing as then an explanation would be needed. If the conversation grows I'll explain my passion is poetry and travel.

Yes, I'm sane

I answer: 'I work as a Safety Advisor in the gas and oil industry, though seldom this year.'

'You aren't going to go back to work?' Veronica asks.

It's not a career.

'What about money?'

'I have enough to satisfy my children my wife for the time being.'

'Are you still writing poetry?'

How about you ~~fuck~~ me and I'll write a poem about it.

'Nobody reads poetry,' I answer.

I think she reads poetry.

'I remember, you read poetry, you like poetry. Maybe you write poetry?' I ask her.

Veronica. 'Yes I read and write poetry – I enjoy both – an enjoyment. You treat it as life and death and I just enjoy it.'

She is the smart one – too smart. You can be too smart.

She'd hold me for a weekend. I'd comfort her – sounds foolish, sounds fascinating. That was Veronica and I.

Here she is brushing against me, staring, laughing at my sayings – her sparkling brown eyes, her light tanned skin blushing as much as it can. And what do I think? I think give me a ride to the store.

Slender and free, more muscle now, no need for children or a husband – she owns her house, her business, her car, and her vacation home at the ski resort. Let us not get carried away, she isn't rich but she does well in a small town.

She was married for two years. He spent her money. She cheated. Divorced.

She considered having a child – never found the father is all.

Here I am.

'So ~~Motherfucker~~, here you are' is what she must think.

'What do you miss about me?' she asks.

Long nights.

What will we do now?

'Are you going to stay in Lake Wapa for awhile?'

Yes – I will stay for a while, I think.

'Come see me.'

I hesitate.

'Just come, you'll see. Come fast – on Monday I'm home.'

'I haven't a car.' I laugh.

'I'll pick you up.'

I can use my mother's I suppose.

I don't ask her if she is married or engaged – I don't ask her a question I know the answer to. She was seeing someone, is seeing someone, or will be seeing someone.

They call the inventors of the atom bomb genius – and I question that maybe there was a better invention they missed, maybe evil championed this invention and buried truly genius ideas. Dreamer is my career, Realist my job. They gave the Noble Peace Prize in the 1970's for the bombing of people, animals, nature, and nests. As wicked of an animal that ever stood, this society disguised as good.

A bright sun has shone with a dark moon. I can manage this luster if I move on before the blue moon.

Sex is our ruler . . . Affection our enemy.

She begs my head.

It doesn't matter her name – go to a place and meet a woman – a story will come.

Chips in our body. They say some of our cells aren't real, not human, not alive, dead objects are perhaps already in our body – living cells fight the machines inside – is it true? Non-living in our body manipulating us. Perhaps we are just animals with machinery inside, making us the top fake ape.

My hands automatically go. I can't stop myself – I'm encrypted – I'm living – I'm vile – I have no name – I put words on a computer screen.

I want to forget desire – I can write about women and adventure my whole life every day, this is nothing, beautiful is all. Ugly is something.

I have no occupation, nothing. There is nowhere I can go – this is the world.

What to write if I can't write expected fantasy. Can't write complain, can't write about taboo, can't write misadventure – how to write?

Perfect, fleeting impossible, and then one-minute, one-hour, one-day, perfect.

End it there, quit.

Hammer – smashing through the reflective mirror. Evolve. I have no use for device, I be human – universe. What you build is a cheat to what we already possess.

'You drink beer?' My old friends will say – they remember I didn't drink when I left.

Nope, no beer – I like it intravenously – like a direct line to the brain. Quick, not too violent. Enough to feel it, disobey it, and then forget it, fall asleep on it.

Quick, quiet, strong.

I hate drinking, it is the legal choice we have.

They say you need to get laid and that will stop a person from drinking but when I get laid I like to have a drink afterwards reflect on the sex and let the height of euphoria prolong into the buzz of a drink. And that buzz can lead to another drink the next day – I might not get laid but I'll manipulate the feeling with a drink.

Is God an animal or a PowerStation? That's next week - this week I verse Hangover as I'm the one competing... and you'll be spectator.

Go cheer for hangover – I'll be underdog. You can hope . . . Hair of the dog, a delayed hangover on the road to a streak of abuse.

If my body is ill my mind is doing well. If my body is fine my mind is poor.

Comfortable – we say at work, never get comfortable as something will go wrong.

At least at work I don't drink.

Lazy streamer black caffeine hiding waiting knowing – my body not giving me happy, not giving me strength knowing I'm poor and can't afford a chi latte – tea will have to do.

Verse, Prose, Poetry.

I don't want them.

Can I have in-between?

It was said there are only two ways to communicate

Prose or poetry = (I say) fake, polished, over valued.

My friend, the published author has received a grant to write – he's received thirty thousand dollars to write a second novel. He received fifty thousand from his publisher for his first novel and yet he still works with me in the oil field, taking care of his family first and writing second, even though writing is first writing is always first.

Work is a small memory of laughter. My author friend is not part of my Ruins – I will see him in the future. I'm reading wonderful scenes in his new manuscript, it is the opposite direction I'm headed. I've been writing something far away from a novel. He's been scolding me to write a two-hundred-fifty-page novel. Take everything I've been writing and decide on a story. It would be a turn around. It would be as they say a project on top of a project on top of project. It would be taking three half-built homes and sliding them together into a livable home.

I know my author friend is trying to help. He may or may not know my Machine is broken.

Writing is the world's most dangerous profession; you can do it in ill health or tripping, you can search heartbreak, adventure, torture, you can accept poverty, you can summon peril, all in verse. No schedule no place. 'A Poet' god-bless them – poetry is a dead-end pure strength pursuit.

My author friend says, 'Only a few people can write a book – very few. So pursue it, write, as you are one that can write – you are a genius – you don't understand that very few people can write. Don't stop, don't waste a day, a minute...write.' He is the smartest man yet he is lost in the bay of a mindless job instead of living, still his life is at work because at home, much like me, it is alone – family and alone because this is where we can produce. No time for living, just produce thoughts to paper.

I call him.

'Where are you? When are you coming to work?' he asks.

'I have a new job.'

'What's the job?'

'Extorting – extortion. That's all I can tell you.'

'Will you not be using violence?' he chuckles.

Only a violent mind.

'How much will you be extorting?'

'First, I have to change my being... become mean and do what I think is best, not what I'm supposed to think is best – not listen to others is all I can say. I need to change my aura, my being, my future, my past – change my skin.'

'Are you sure about this?'

'Sure.'

'Are you experienced in extortion?'

'Yes, extortion has been used against me.'

'Why extort? You could just go back to work.'

'I'm working now. I don't want to work in a job I distain.'

'Yes, writing is work, correct. But at this time you are not getting paid to write. You get paid working in the oil and gas industry.'

'I'm not quitting, just taking time off. I will be back to work in the spring.'

'You better not kill someone.'

Oh someone will be dead – but they won't have a face.

I have to answer the question about going back to work everyday, to every visitor that comes to my mother's house, every relative I talk on the phone, and every person I run into on the street. I'm good at it, avoiding answering the question without many inquires.

The label – you are what you work. My label is 'the safety guy'. How misplaced.

My agenda always the same: write, stay in shape, try not to have a career.

—

Unlike me, Veronica never speaks in riddles. She isn't always true – I didn't know this until she was mean to me. Mean is a trick to bring about love. She was mean with words because I was in her head – I could hurt her.

Go ahead and ~~fuck~~ is what our Master would tell us.

I know we won't. If we did we wouldn't stop. Sometimes you have a friend, and friends do the same thing over and over again – if we never touch, we never touch, if we touch we touch.

She can talk, argue, some prefer to say debate.

I think debate.

She's offered me a room in her basement which sounds good. Veronica is a neat freak; her home and yard are well kept although her main floor has become more like a huge office than a home. A tidy, delightful office.

She's offered me a job as a temporary safety for her company.

'Give me a hundred and fifty for water, power, wear and tear. – You see, it isn't free, just cheap.'

'What else?'

'Nothing. You can work part-time for me at my company. The pay won't be much but you have a place to stay and a vehicle to drive.'

'Yes, I want to start today.'

'Tomorrow. Part-time. When I say go, you go check what I need checked,' she laughs, insane.

Yes to everything.

I don't know why Veronica is doing this – perhaps our friendship or it's possible she just needs part-time help with her company.

Veronica calls across the room to her assistant. 'Neha, come met our new errand boy and houseguest.'

Neha walks over, sits down. She is in her late twenties, maybe early thirties, polite, quiet. Red lip-stick, little makeup. Dark sultry shoulder-length hair pulled back – jeans and white blouse – average height, in shape, looks nice.

Veronica resumes instructions. 'Monday through Friday eight through four-thirty Neha will be here doing office work and tidying up. Be nice to her.'

I nod. I certainly will be nice.

'This safety position in the company. It is a made-up position. Neha and I prefer to work at my home as opposed to the office

– we already have a receptionist at the office – less distractions here. I need somebody to check up on my drivers and deliveries to clients. It's a supervisory position. You will only answer to Neha and myself. You are extra help and extra eyes. I can promise you work for a few months but make it worth my while and at least stay on for a month until I hire and train a couple of Supervisors. We do neighborhood and industrial patrol, resort patrol, residential, property security, and cyber security. Provide security equipment. You'll need to check the vehicles are cleaned and inspected, check all the security paperwork is filled out just like you do in the oil field – make sure everyone is doing their job. You're my safety. Don't worry, everyone will be scared of you because you are working directly for me. You won't have to give any direction, just relay information to me and Neha – bypass my supervisors unless we direct you to communicate to them.'

'Do I work night shift, day shift, or both?'

'Day shift, I have enough staff on night shift – it is day shift I have the problem. It is a good job – you'll like it. You don't even have to wear a uniform, just wear our sport jacket with our logo. I know you L Ce I've created employment for you. Smile. Run around, sit around.'

Veronica is good. I've never had to pester her, mislead, cheat, nor stuck to hold my word until the truth came bursting out in a dissatisfied parade.

Here I am today benefiting from the pleasure of time I'd spent with her. It all turns around they say; spend the time and it will spend back on you someday.

Veronica disappears into the office with Neha to prepare a contract for me to sign.

In less than a week Veronica's assistant Neha will be some kind of burning fire, some kind of healing spirit, her golden indo skin, her elegant ways. She is surely no princess, more of a woman who served a princess – so quiet, delicate, a delight. Living art. I don't want to break her; I break the ones who are broken.

Everything has happened quickly.

I could have stayed at my mother's as was my plan but Veronica's place comes with a company van – minus $150 per month and a low rate of pay – perfect.

Her house is late eighties style redone, two upper floor bedrooms. Half the basement stores her business products, files, and the other half is my living quarters with all the necessities. Fine for the price, a job, and possible entertainment.

———

After Veronica's I meet with the Trustee I've chosen about debt.

I drove, I phoned, I walked in, I walked out – it took me a week to feel the right trustee to trust with a solution for my debt.

My final choice, I knew as soon as I walked in and made an appointment, was not the most popular place.

Now I'm back for my appointment.

I don't have to do anything. I walk in and say, 'I'm broke.'

The trustee is pleasant, she stands in front of me shaking her head at the banks. She understands the live in debt set up.

How much in debt she asks next

One hundred and twenty thousand dollars.

The bank lent money to a man that has no collateral, no sufficient funds, no backing as they say. They kept offering money and I kept saying yes and now I can't make the payments because they've stopped lending – if they hadn't have stopped lending I'd kept receiving.

I don't have to wait long for the last question, 'What did you do with the money?' She's dead serious.

I'm not. I don't care what she'll believe.

Travel, I say. Writing a book.

'Oh,' she nods.

There is no way to recapture something that is spent on experience.

The rest is easy; a bad year, a reduction in pay rate. I only made 35% of what I usually make in a year.

'You were making close to a hundred thousand dollars a year before this year. That is a lot of money,' she states.

It is I suppose.

I can't make that kind of money at this time, I tell her – and it is true – I'm considering a different career, I'm just not clear what new avenue that will be.

She listens, then adds up my current employment conditions.

Bankruptcy can be avoided.

I can make a proposal to pay back a portion of the money I owe.

'What assets do you have?'

None.

'Home?'

No.

'Car?'

No car.

'Where do you stay, lease rent?'

I stay with a friend, family, or at work in a camp or hotel, rent is minimal.

'Assets? Investments?'

No assets, no investments.

'Pension?'

Pension is locked in from work. I still collect benefits from work as well even when I'm not working.

'That's good – that is really good. They can't touch that. Married?'

'Yes, to a non-resident, she lives overseas.'

'Children?'

'Three. Overseas.'

'You send money home?'

It goes like that.

'Okay. What about expenses?'

None but the money I owe.

'Phone? How much income a month, take home?'

I explain my new part-time job as safety for a security firm.

She retreats to her note-pad, then to another room.

She returns and says, 'Okay, I will make a proposal to creditors that you will pay $300.00 a month interest free for five years or until you pay eighteen thousand dollars back, which-ever comes first. The other one hundred and two thousand you owe, the banks will eat.

I almost smile. My eyes certainly gleam.

'Can you handle the payments?'

Yes – I may find my way back to my regular work and can have this paid off in a year.

'You could,' she says. 'I'll see what they say. Come back in a week, we'll sign the papers. I must also see proof of everything you said as soon as possible. I need documentation.'

When I get back to Mother's my phone rings – I pick up the cheap cell phone without looking at the number.

Dispatch from work calling to ask if I'm available for work.

I say, no.

'When will you be available?'

In two months, if you have a good job.

It is necessary to find a job that pays enough to get by yet gives me time to pursue other ventures. My job in the oil field pays too much and the bank might take my wages and prefer bankruptcy.

Employment with Veronica is perfect.

I have to thank Veronica a million times.

I can only repay Veronica with thought.

You can't ask to be a teacher or a student, a teacher is only a teacher and a student is only a student – they are words not an action, it just happens... like love.

I won't tell you my scheme, my system. I wouldn't tell you how I won so why would I tell you how I lost?

Recognition and accomplishment aren't the same.

I knew the result before I began – it was the steps taken to get here that was and is the adventure, the torture. Would I be the same... again I knew I would never be the same as I was when I made the decision.

You have to have a story – the human lie machine always has a story.

—

Screws

'Screws' – a dispatch to the 'Screw' and all that have encountered them. What brought about this event, a Screw I met on a job, like Frankenstein – he turned the screws inside the employees' heads, controlling them, breaking them, and eventually he created monsters and the employees turned on him. And I remembered all the Screws I'd met.

I never knew what the word Screw meant, it was a tool to me – and then I'd heard 'Screw off', still it didn't have deep meaning it was just a rougher 'Get lost' or a nicer 'F-off". And I couldn't miss 'Good screw' – again this took me a long while to understand.

A Unit Manger inspecting workers performance – critiquing, explaining, testing, insulting, and most of all applying extreme pressure to the workers minds, then releasing before applying pressure again until their brain's began to tighten in frustration to the point of exploding.

The Unit Manager enjoyed this screwing because he could for as long and hard as he wanted.

He knew the workers weren't in a position to quit.

Later the Unit Manager walked up to me and said, 'Do you love your job?'

Confirmation I was dealing with a Screw.

He wasn't human at all. He was a Beast. I'd think Alien but that would be demeaning to an Alien, as Aliens might be intelligent.

The Screws aren't smart – they are imposters.

More beast than human.

The Screws are only presenting itself as man.

They appear ultra nice, it is their way to gain trust, but there is a time limit.

A Screw can only play the concerning human until it has a situation of control – have you cornered, and then the screws come out and you are ...you got it – screwed.

They rise to a position of power where they can install screws to your head, past your mind to your brain – don't let this happen. Stop them at your mind and play Frankenstein. Let them believe it, play them to your advantage. All the while pretending you enjoy the support of the Screws.

Flashes of the Beast occurred in the Unit Manager. When he smiled, if you looked past the gap you saw it wasn't a smile but a growl – as Screws really aren't able to smile, his hands grasped together salivating – greed. I could read his thoughts, his inner self. Not human and worse than a Beast. A Beast at least doesn't know any better, but the Screw is conscious of the mean instinct that it serves.

Whatever favors the Screw gives, you'll pay it back ten times. The Screw will never leave you alone. They follow you, save you, hope that you crave them, because they've positioned themselves to flourish with your help. They've shorted you of everything but offer the only rope you can grab to help yourself out of the jam they lead you into.

The Screw save's and swallows. They destroy all other possibilities around you. All that real green grass you so deserve, destroyed by an imposter.

Start fresh and slowly you'll grow to success.

I've had some fantastic mangers in my different jobs through life – I've used this manager as an example.

A Screw could be anyone.

It is a foreign object thwarting pleasure, it will never give you what you want; freedom of mind, freedom of space.

My first revelation of the word Screw of the good kind – was with a fine woman one magnificent morning.

Someone somewhere experienced the same insight as I and called it screwing.

Fitting.

4

―――

I WAIT FOR VERONICA for some kind of performance. We are distant – delaying something to go wrong, delaying something to go right. It occurs to me that I have stopped thinking about Veronica.

My new job is easy, perfect really as I can make time to write. Making money to write you could say. I've been writing for a couple hours each day between duties.

I have been laughing with Neha daily. Our first day alone was wonderful and we ate dinner together before she went home. I couldn't sleep that night thinking the perfect position I'd been afforded.

Neha and I drink tea side by side, our chairs touching. It has become our routine to have afternoon tea together.

Veronica joins, she sits across the table from us – small talk with Neha.

Neha pulls off her shoe, stretches her foot above mine. Her toe ring is impressive – each toe stretched – striking my pant leg with the edge of her foot, then it is over, her foot back in her shoe. Her hair flung loose then wrapped again – Veronica unaware? – I'm aware.

A glimpse of her naked foot, toes – smell – if you like their odor you'll react – I like her odor. This is where it will end, this is what we are after, to dose in each other's odors – Neha wooed me, why?

To shout daily for romantic, or is it real – it isn't real she has children, a home, a husband, a job, a family, and I will be something for her, for herself – if I ruin her life . . . she won't respond.

Neha, I could report her, her flirtatiousness as playful harassment. I, the man, stay my balance and don't say a word, or words, or touch the wrong place – I don't deserve to stay quiet. 21st century man has to be given the permission to go ahead, seduce. Neha, I have this permission. Neha, I will not let you get away. It is my day off tomorrow – I can be near you.

—

I didn't have any authors as influences when growing up. I've always read. I spent a lot of time in the school library. I'd even skip class and hid out in the library. I'd mostly read information on people, places, and events. I read a novel with a backdrop of ice hockey, my favorite sport. I think I was eight or nine years of age. I was so disappointed in the description of the ice hockey scenes that I decided someday I would write a book, as I felt you didn't have to be perfect or good to make it into the library. I wish someone had told me being good has nothing to do with being in the library. All you need is work, luck, or money.

I learned from the author Henry Miller – he'd tell his wife he was at home writing while she was at work even though he was sleeping, reading, drinking, walking, or perhaps entertaining.

I love it. Morning through afternoon at home writing – my wife will say, "What do you do all day?"

Everything, I'll say.

When writing begins, it begins, what happens after that, I don't know . . . kinda of like talking.

It is impossible to explain to someone that you are working when you are waiting for inspiration to arrive.

If I say, 'What a day I'm exhausted.'

They'll say, 'Tired from what?'

But if they went to the gym or cleaned the yard working muscles of the body, they can claim, 'I'm tired, what a work-out.'

Mother of all...

Don't kid yourself.

Imagination is a workout.

—

Neha doesn't come into work today ... her child is taking the day off from school. I cover for her on my day off, some administrative work, my delivery duties. It is my worst day, no writing, no enjoyment, only painful duties. I won't see Neha till Monday.

If I drink I need to obliterate my mind – put a mark on my soul. Ruin my body and let it cure.

Sometimes I'm productive if I drink the night before because I haven't fear or anxiety. I relax selfish.

Our modern technical advances are already inside us, already present in the universe. We are traveling to the beginning. How do I harness this message? Stay quiet don't speak. Have it proven by a paid scientist, go preach it, cult the revolution – or pass the word from ear to ear, or have I fallen victim to drama, a comfort instilled in my head, a protection claiming there is more to life and death?

For now, for today, my message is the same. Yes, an opposite message will also be sought and after time a leaning will sway. I have no value, no struggle for my thoughts, tomorrow it can change and I may be guided to a completely different theory. If one could accumulate many theories of life they may have a reasonable question. Problem is humanity is not flexible – the 'I believe in this' is instilled and can't be changed even when fought.

Blood, nationality, and belief keep making the same mistake

You want to live life a certain way = live it! Don't brag it, don't flog it. Just make a good an example of it.

Restart tradition. Bring in some outside influence. Take your beliefs to the next level. Combine or shut your mouth and live the results.

Veronica and I would spend magnificent hours together – her shirt pulled up, her pants pulled down. Now does she want to finish it, to complete our sexual hostility?

I have lied; we did finish and she pulled me, striking me with all her power. She did complete many times and I did, I did enter her house years after our first encounter.

So we don't have to go any further. We weren't lovers. We stayed still after this encounter and we pulled each other maybe a couple of more times – still it was friends, always friends. I miss a friend like this with a chance for anything or nothing or something in between, to have jealousy without reason, to have secrets, to do things nobody will or would understand in a relationship with forbidden closeness.

This morning Veronica asks, 'How is the writing going?'

What I've wrote before was up-tempo joyful and what I write now is exaggerated severe apocalyptic – I can't combine them – it is two different languages even though the message is the same.

'You were happy when you wrote before, and now you are not.'

'No, it isn't that; it is two different styles, same story.'

'Are you sure you're happy?'

I'm not happy now and I didn't consider myself happy before, but I wanted to believe I was happy – fake happy. I was writing desperate – throwing sentences in the air, I wanted a break – I wanted an audience. I wanted to show how good life was and now I don't believe my life is great now or great then. I'm in admittance.

'You want to get the story right. What is the story about?'

'Nothing, no country, no culture, no place, just Earth.'

Before I wanted to write with the sounds of the brain beating invisible signals of blood running – swearing and dreaming thinking out loud. A lot of swearing, a lot of sex, a lot of nonsense. I wrote what people thought, what people said.

Now I still want to swear, write sex, and a lot of nonsense except now I don't write to the beats of my blood, the sound of my brain – I write to the pulse of machine.

Veronica and I can laze around together all day – walk the park, have breakfast. Veronica is tall enough, she is plain enough, but I don't want it.

I ask Veronica if she has time to drive over to my friend Tru's and he in return can drive me back.

She agrees to take me over to Tru's.

I never mixed Tru and Veronica in the past, only discussed them in passing conversation; they belong to different worlds.

On the drive to Tru's home Veronica asks, 'Doesn't he deal drugs or do drugs?'

'I don't think so. In the past he may have. He runs, snowmobiles, swims, rides bicycle in the summer. He can afford to drink and take drugs in moderation but he doesn't drink excessively – too many mistakes – he doesn't like to fail.'

'Fail at what?' she thinks out loud.

'Whatever he does.'

'What does he do?'

'Invest in friend's business.'

'I see.' She sounds dissatisfied.

'You want to know about our friendship?' I ask.

'Yes.'

He quotes my quotes, tells others who think I'm weird that they aren't at my level of thought. He'd ask me to recite famous quotes. If persons threatened me, he'd threaten them. We used to snowboard, play Ping Pong, and go out at night. He'd invite me to cruise the lake on his boat.

Everything I've spoken good about Tru is gone in an instant as we turn into Tru's alley.

I'd asked Veronica to drive around to the back alley as I could see Tru's ferocious dog running lose, barking in the front yard.

Instantly – a show – no script – I don't know what Veronica thinks – my speech dissolved.

A machete in hand, Tru stands surrounded by a crowd of twelve in the alley. A man in his thirties stands in defensive posture with a 3ft metal scaffolding pipe, backing away from Tru, towards us. Veronica stops the car.

I tell Veronica to keep the car running, lock the doors.

Clash clang, the machete bangs the pipe.

Repeat, clash clang – the metals join like a movie fight.

I feel calm. I don't feel Tru will be hurt or strike the man with his machete – I have no inclination to get out of the car; the scene is unbelievable and I want no part of it – ancient practice – the man with the pipe is frightened – frightened enough that he is more likely to strike than Tru. I believe Tru is aware of this too as Tru's strikes to the metal pipe are more aimed at the pipe than the man.

The onlookers of twelve are almost silent. None of them are attempting to intervene. Two children – a couple of teenagers – six male adults ranging from twenty-one to sixty years old, and two women mid-thirties, I'd say. Two more male adults enter the alley from a backyard in the immediate area of the action.

Seems the confrontation has been going on for sometime.

Twice more, metals clash.

'What about the police?' Veronica asks.

Nobody will call the police – or capture this on their phones.

'Is the guy with the pipe his friend?'

I don't know. I only recognize four people and they are all Tru's friends, or were Tru's friends.

You never know with friends; once in a while friends fight after many laughs.

As Tru backs away the man with the pipe picks up a brick from a pile next to a garbage container and throws the brick at Tru, forcing distance between them. The man grabs another brick, throwing it as he runs through an open backyard gate and slams the gate closed behind him. Tru doesn't chase.

The man runs to the back street, enters a car, and drives away.

Tru holds court, enjoying – exciting the viewers with as much astonishment as them of the action scene.

Tru walks towards Veronica's car and recognizes me. Laughs, comments, 'Some people just don't appreciate favors,' referring to the gentleman he just had the confrontation with.

He says hi to Veronica. 'Would you mind giving me a lift?'

Veronica smiles 'If it is okay with L Ce.'

It is okay with me.

We leave the alley.

Tru directs. 'There is a small pizza joint just up the Highway. Can you take me there?'

What happened, what we witnessed is not discussed.

Tru invites us in for pizza.

Veronica and Tru talk bicycling. He has a mountain bike for sale – new, never used. He says he bought the mountain bike for his girlfriend but she left him before he had a chance to gift it to her.

Tru motions, 'Here's my ride,' as he nods to a man near the entrance. Tru asks the server for the bill and to box his pizza for takeaway. He pays for our orders and leaves. 'Stop by again,' he says to me.

Veronica and I enjoy pizza but we do not talk until we return to her car.

'I hope you don't owe him a favor?' she comments.

'No, he owes me many favors. At best we are even.'

'That doesn't sound very refreshing. Are you sure he isn't a drug dealer?' Veronica questions.

He isn't a drug dealer. He makes friends and then helps them out; he'd buy a house and have friends pay the rent for him, he'd invest in things that someone else wanted to own if they didn't have the money. He'd make money without doing anything, on the fringe of breaking the law. I can't even explain it. I don't know what he does now other than he rents out his homes.

'He beats people up. That is against the law. He is a loan shark. That is against the law.'

'You know more about him than I do,' I laugh.

He doesn't beat people up. He finds other ways to get his money.

'He steals.'

No, he is creative.

'He has never been in jail?'

'He has but not prison.'

'I thought he didn't break the law?'

'We all break the law. Too much talk – drive.'

'You want to protect him.'

I'd protect you too.

Her last question is, 'Am I going to be safe having you staying in my home?'

It is something to walk through your Ruins – fear of what they all have, the same fear as seeing me as 'The Visitor'.

I'm satisfied – I don't have them both, Tru and Veronica in the same room so I can tell each the secrets I like.

Most of my friends in this town aren't like this. They are normal, normal as children, normal adults. I know many . . . what can I say? They have their lives – my life has past.

—

The Human Being

Walk on water – rise above a scene

Black

Light

Simple

You have the middle, unaware.

Levitation as thought by ancients is forgot today.

Today the practitioner bounces in the lotus position, ha ha ha, I laugh, this is what you call levitation training, funny.

Levitation isn't physical, it is your matter, your being levitating – the invisible you levitating (what-ever you are).

Free your mind – let imagination find.

I don't know if thoughts on magic mushrooms are real.

I consumed magic mushrooms many times, each time an interestingly extraordinaire feeling – levitation, or out an of body experience seemed to occur on one of these trips.

About an hour after a co-worker and I began tripping we entered a pub to meet up with some co-workers from the railway gang I was traveling and working on.

Nineteen years old.

Unable to speak, let alone communicate, to the five other co-workers sitting on stools at a table about to have dinner. Disconnected from my earthly being, I was desperately trying to travel back to my physical self so I could resume an earthly function, as I was not sure if I were able to say yes or no if asked a question.

I truly thought I was gone from prior feelings of what life was. I was afraid my co-workers might find that I wasn't in an organic shell any longer.

I was traveling invisible, my mind, my matter, and my unknown levitating beyond my physical self – a new pinnacle. My feet still flat on the floor, my being levitated, tilted forward better than a half a meter off the ground and a half-meter away from were my feet stayed grounded. It wasn't as if I was looking back at myself – I'd truly just moved to a better vantage point of the scene without my physical self moving from where I stood. Levitation, astral plane, out-of-body experience, or just a hallucination, it was out of this world.

The trip ended sometime that evening, back to the organic shell.

I woke up the next morning and went to work on the rail gang I was employed with. Nobody mentioned anything unordinary other than my friend who was also tripping. He said to me, 'You were really fucked up last night,' and then he smiled. 'I was fucked up too!' The mushrooms were from the majestic forest of Queen Charlotte Island.

Substance stories are like love and heartbreak tales.

~~Fuck~~ I could talk about the buzz of tea, the emotional jilt of coffee. I say jilt, as coffee is always the complete let down, robust freeze. Tea the lingering forget.

Never touch speed (ice) methamphetamine – wreck your mind, body, soul, plus the unknown.

Really, no need to touch anything, but if you are going to burn your body with alcohol you might want to relax with something else.... end of tell you want to do today.

Stories of miracles, super powers, and spiritual texts – I'm just debunking them, relating to them, understanding them, and recreating them.

By the way, stay away from hard drugs, prescription or otherwise, just saying, and if you do find the right conditions, have some control.

'Shut up,' I can hear you say. I ask Machine: 'Why do I need to bring that stuff up?'

If you want to talk about life you must study bad as much as good.

I ask Machine why I've talked about drugs and mushrooms – Machine says, 'If you are to tell a story of life you must include drugs.'

Drugs are not entertainment. Drugs take away entertainment.

Drugs welcome you with open arms – hello, you are okay, comfortable, so comfortable we will not let you leave easily.

If you use drugs to experience otherworld, you aren't in touch. You haven't experience.

Relax, all the drug does is bring out what you already have, and if it brings something new in you are destroying the part that was already there, that you hadn't accessed naturally. If you don't like something about yourself you'll conceal it with a drug.

Drugs just make what I've always felt worse.

Ha, ha, ha, the joke of life:

Create, don't mask.

Write what my mind thinks – danger lurks – our thoughts monitored and the new being is born, besting religion.

How about a drug to subdue thoughts, to protect mankind for thinking the wrong things? This would solve free thought and then we could still have free speech as no wrongs would or could be spoken.

A society free of decadent thought, free of hate – you can't have one without the other – free of innocence, free of love.

Abolishing choice is abolishing evolution resulting in creation, no individual thought, and no individual voice.

You could say the animal doesn't have choice – it has instinct. You could say the human doesn't have choice, our thoughts conditioned to our surroundings – you haven't free will. Evolved before existence – you haven't choice.

I was to find love, heartbreak, isolation . . . I was created and evolved.

Predetermined.

Let me put it this way:

If you believe in creation = Predetermined.

If you believe we are programmed, if you believe we evolved scientifically, if you believe we are a product of our surroundings = again Predetermined.

If this is the case, I need not to make decisions – my path is decided for me.

Make your plight – random or otherwise.

Select a day and select a belief, what-ever works best for you in the scene of the night – the human lie machine is so convenient.

Yeah experiment.

Experiment. And live the results.

Like the plant sprouting for the light.

When you think you are breathing your last breath, you may see a far away light growing bigger as you pull the rope to alive, until that light gets brighter and you are back in the realm of alive not dead.

I don't know what happens when that faraway light doesn't enlarge or never appears.

You've seen the light

Makes sense doesn't it, the light pulling you awake? So many examples in history.

I'd been in a car accident at fifteen years of age – the driver fifteen years of age too. No driver's license, an early morning drive. Volume loaded, music of the Clash. I don't remember a crash.

The first thing I remember is light, dull, distant, then brighter, – like the opening of an angel's wings. I woke naked, no pain, with a room full of extraterrestrials searching my body. Though it was only hospital staff checking for injuries.

I could relay this story of an angel saving me from death and then extraterrestrial's healing.

Instead I'll keep it real.

The light we seek for comfort.

The ancients were doing this.

They manipulated.

The holy in white will turn the screws hard and not let go until you've given your life away as the messenger, the servant, and then it doesn't matter if your life is good or bad as you have been saved, loved. You've become one with God. Welcome Satan. Sometimes they dress in black with the white of light around their neck or above their head – we all know the light we pull when in need.

The salesmen for spirituality know this, and exploit it. Dress themselves as angels, as stars.

Yes, it is simple, magical art. Go to the light. Go to them. Follow the lighthouse.

Is it a cross, a light, a star, or the sun? Look at it.

Advertising at its best – the best things don't need advertising.

I'm no angel, but yes, when I overindulge I search for light.

So be it.

Go ahead, have fun and repent.

I injected cocaine the last time – lights out, black gone dead – I didn't cry out to God. Me myself and I used all my strength not to cross to the other side. I pulled myself back to earth when I saw a pinhole of a light. After struggle the full light shined.

Cured.

Pass out – find light – born again.

You could always go the Eastern soup opera of religion.

Where does the color red fit in?

Red haze brings on psychedelic colors – stand and observe.

Alien abduction...

I don't ~~fucking~~ know.

—

Dynamic Affect

I don't have technical words or knowledge.

To experience Dynamic Affect is as I wrote the next morning without full understanding of it:

Electric shock therapy last night – no, I didn't hook myself up to electricity. It was all done inside my head. Shocking my brain. Yes, an electrical storm, nullifying nerves, switching circuits, connecting wires.

Burst of scenes flashing in my mind too fast to distinguish what's been deleted – turned off turned on!

I'd been lazy, confidence gone – diet was off.

Bring on the electrical charges, let neuron's flicker in my brain.

About fifty charges last night, that means fifty new patterns, or fifty dissolved, fantastic.

I thought the inventors of shock therapy would be on to this. Some will say I dreamed it from the knowledge of it.

This episode wasn't dreamt.

I treated.

The flashes kept me from dreaming – the sparks could be alarming if you haven't experience, and disarming if you have experience.

I'm not saying I'm a believer in electrical shock therapy; I'm not sponsoring or questioning. I believe in my own therapy. You may have already done it – though you haven't recognized it – plug in – you'll feel zaps of light inside your mind like a trigger switch. Scenes of life disappear and wake.

Flashes in the mind, subtle electrical charges in the body, dulling previous paths and creating new vision to be shone through the mind.

You have to recognize it as positive, not as restless sleep – but as electrical change. You are ready to go, open to the future.

I never recognized that Dynamic Affect was only a setting for transformation; I thought it was transformation. Months passed before I made the connection, when the Lotus Affect came.

—

Lotus Affect

I wasn't physically levitating, star-like matter was; my being.

A cool mix of matter dissolving my body from my feet to my head section by section, feet gone, knee gone, waist gone, leaving only my mind and star-like particles, an invisible man. Several passes occur until energy lifts from my body and levitates slightly above my physical, before returning to my body and the episode is over.

Lotus – mythical, spiritual – you ever wonder why?

Aesthetically pleasing, palatable, enhancing a pond.

Is this why Lotus is admired ... maybe?

Naturally, I thought the Lotus has characteristics to be glorified – supreme. I ate it, grew it, marveled it, took photos – peaceful with a bouquet.

What else did I know? Nothing. I didn't research, infuse the lotus, I was humbled by the usefulness, I judged it by what others had done.

I accepted it significant like I invented the mystic myself. I forgave any flaws and deemed it an important Lilly. That was until realization.

When a healthy realm of energy created my being new, the 'Lotus Affect' I was told by my mind. I'd experienced a modern realization of what some had experienced before – a new being unheeded by past and ready to accept new vision. It is the next level of my being.

I'd talked about my experience of Dynamic Affect and now I've had the organic transportation – maybe the dynamic electricity numbed the past, and the Lotus Affect grows my future.

Let me tell it again slowly. A flow of gentle energy from my feet travels to my head, dissolving my physical being many times in a row. Then star-like matter rises above my being and levitates. The entire scene lasts an unknown amount of time – I'd say in my reality under or over a minute before rejoining with my being.

The best I can deceiver is replacement of particles or spirit matter.

I can explain it in a hundred different ways – I've written and re-wrote.

I was nothing and then something, every single ingredient of my body created I could feel each individual star of creation.

Transformation, creation, transportation, levitation, teleportation.

I can use many words – maybe I'll show you one day, Lotus Affect.

—

What images my mind produced or experienced was mine. Your vision or experience may result in different terminology.

Why should you believe? Society is built on mythical belief.

Now I must learn to walk through my Ruins.

Perhaps electricity empowered the star-like particles to recreate.

Do Lotus Affect and Dynamic Affect have a relation? Any man or woman can make a connection, concoct a scheme, write a text, theorize a formula – I really can't say.

We could fill a book with our so-called miracles.

Dynamic Affect and Lotus Affect occurred months before my Fathers death – as I plotted the bank. I was seven-months sober, neither illegal nor legal drugs interfered – complete focus.

Like a fire that scorches the ground, the soil is fertile for new life.

Sleep is where life is made – sometimes energy is so powerful that we are conscious when our life is transforming, we see it in our mind and feel it in our body. If you have restless sleep take it as a positive – maybe you are lit up for a higher level of state.

How to achieve this state?

Get mad – listen. When your mind is ready, your body will follow.

Achieving this state is not the miracle, it is recognizing, harnessing, and evolving.

If you think it happens fast (Lightning and Levitation) you may be disappointed. It can take many fans to stoke smoke to flame or just one. Same goes for growth – the season has to be right. In the phase of growth you must avoid predators, and disasters. You could numb the past and find yourself worse, but why would you create change if it was to be worse? I don't know, but nothing will be easy – finding truth.

If Dynamic is a full mind and body charge,

Lotus is a full mind and body change.

Charge and change.

Your mind is cleaned and your body is ready to redeem.

Electrical signals are all around us – I'm using electricity to write this.

I know walking through my Ruins will have to be next before I can reach another level of spiritual being.

I'm documenting my Ruins now.

5

PROOF HAS BEEN PROVIDED to the Debt Trustee. I sign the papers, agree to make payments of three hundred dollars for five years – no interest – with the option of paying off the eighteen thousand earlier if I like. The creditors cannot reject the deal once they've agreed unless I miss three payments.

I write a creative version of costs.

'It will be tight,' she says. 'I think the creditors will agree but they have the choice to reject the proposal – you understand.'

I understand.

'Eighteen thousand with no interest is pretty good compared to a hundred and twenty thousand plus interest owed.'

'You're right. Thank you.'

'When will you go to Asia to see your family?'

When I have money.

She comments, 'It must be difficult to be away from your children.'

The sadness I feel away from my children is not as great as the happiness when I see them.

'The creditors have forty days to respond. You will hear before sixty days if they have accepted or renegotiated. If they do not agree, they have a total of sixty days starting from today to state in which direction they'd like to proceed. They could also investigate you.'

She seems sad, I seem sad, because now we must wait – the chances are better than 80% the agreement will not be challenged. But there is always a chance.

She is telling me to stay quiet.

I certainly won't go work in the oil field until after forty days have passed.

I pay the trustee first month, plus a fee. I have six weeks to remain cool – no heavy income till then, it isn't worth it.

Three hundred a month won't be easy on my current income – true.

—

I know nothing. I speculate I observe. I've learned to dislike the English language; the sound of it hurts my ears. I may prefer to speak a new way. I speak a lot, I used to speak little. May I please be quiet again.

Neha quiet – almost silent – a fresh channel. I will not attempt to write about a lovely woman; the greatest poets have already done it.

English a language that they say if you see it backwards you have an illness – maybe you were born for a language that goes the opposite direction – after all English is just an invention, doesn't mean it is correct.

I'm in Neha's car as the passenger going to the market. She is no longer quiet – she is thrilling, opinionated laughing and most of all, touching.

For three days we glance, scent, work hard, proud, confident, we agree on everything.

I find my room at the end of the workweek. Neha has come to my door to speak.

Her golden skin is too precious, too sensuous to disappoint.

'Why have you come back to Lake Wapa?' Neha asks.

I want to pursue something.

'Pursue Veronica,' Neha blushes.

No, not Veronica – never Veronica. Something else.

'And your wife? What about your wife?'

Nothing. Here is here, there is there. I will be dealt consequence – perhaps reward for happiness, charmed for teaching, and gather a life for a lit healed heart.

It has started – our desire is no longer, future is our quest.

Quiet. Standing looking directly at me, waiting in her natural perfume for what appears to be a hug as her arms stretch out. My desire escapes, my head tilts as we grasp. My lips absorb the skin of her neck – exquisite – her flourishing sweat leaps to my flavor. A match, a mix, a hunger that could ruin or save my life.

Neha hurries away, turning, smiling. 'I come back on Monday.'

Neha. Her hazel eyes – long dark lashes – soft body, soft skin. She needn't run a marathon or perform all day aerobics – she's in shape but she needn't muscle. She's perfectly charming, plainly sensual. She is no model, she is no hot body, she is no sexy girl, she is no cutie. She is soft mind blowing! Adoring! Hold her for a million miles, taste her for a thousand days, never ever let her out of the house. Her husband is reckless – foolish – perhaps he'd lose her if he never let her out of the house. Maybe he is the greatest lover, the smartest man to have this divine beauty. Perhaps she is trickery – perhaps she is ill, perhaps I'm a fool – because why has she allowed me to taste her neck, to lick, to slobber, to wet my month on her skin? Why didn't I smooch her aloud and take her lips?

You can never say having an affair is safe even if you think it is unlikely your spouse will ever find out. You don't know the unseen, unknown factors, follow me. Call it cause and effect – karma – or just the fact that your spouse is inside you, and you're inside her – we've become one through our children, my spit, is her spit. You have to think my wife's cells can read my cells, my organisms greeting hers with truth, lies, or maybe nothing at all.

Believe what you believe. I'm no angel, a prince, no. (who would want to be).

I'd opportunities more than usually when my wife was pregnant and I never would have been caught, though I can't say never, could have been a disease, a phone call – pregnancy – beaten by a boyfriend–husband, attacked by the woman I'm having the affair with, who knows, a car accident together.

None of which stopped me from a romantic encounter.

So many scenarios you must think. Or you can act without thought, and accept hysteria.

I never went beyond heavy breathing and then I'd vacate, let the woman chase. Feel good about myself. Passing the test.

We live our lives unaware that we produce results with previous indiscretions.

The reason I never succumbed to an external romantic encounter is the unseen, the unknown. I felt it was not the right time with my wife being pregnant with our daughter.

A voice in my mind, a voice in my heart: 'Don't do anything wrong, our daughters health will be risked.'

And that was my reasoning – more than reasoning, my honest belief. My reward if I didn't cheat would be a beautiful healthy daughter.

As a man, I was tested with marriage offers, affairs, and afternoon rendezvous.

That voice in my mind stopped me.

My daughter was born, more beautiful than I'd imagined. Have faith – my system worked, faithful, healthy, and happy!

Yes, I'll never know the truth if I'd preceded with a romantic encounter, but what if I'm right, and the detractors wrong?

—

Doesn't matter the name of religion – I know they'll tell you they are not all the same.

As a boy I refused to go back to Sunday school after one try.

I cried when I was a boy at church and maybe I wasn't wrong, but to be truly sure to argue it to the eighth degree with fries – to legally debate with tea – I needed to witness it.

In the past Veronica invited me to church.

I went five times. I read I listened, I debated. I had an affair with an unhappily married woman. Veronica resolves I must confess. I confess to the Bishop – thankful I'm put on probation.

Veronica happy, I happy, the Bishop happy, unhappily married woman not so happy I ended the affair.

No more church.

Church was good; I experienced, I sought what I needed.

I no longer needed to debate spiritual religion – I no longer get up to argue. I just listen. I have no debate. I have no cross-examination – it is too plain to discuss Santa Clause at Christmas with a child … protect the weak. Let them figure it out themselves.

Veronica is in and out of church – holidays she's in, trouble she's in, break up's she's in – romance she's out, summer time she's out… I'm her friend.

Passionate Neha: 'Veronica said you are very kind. I know you will be kind to me too.'

A slow drawbridge above the moat.

What is kind Veronica? My past is now present.

What kind of man am I to have this Neha – this sudden attraction, this sudden leave my wife?

I cannot have you. I cannot afford you. I would be the saddest man... a life living for money and dying for jealousy.

Kill her, love now, attack her, hurt her feelings so she'll never hold my hand again.

Is she willing to destroy my family?

Am I willing to destroy hers?

Laughable, are these thoughts.

Why a beautiful woman? I ask every day for a beautiful woman, but not one that brings me the pain of lust, only innocent fun.

How many questions will I ask – keep asking, keep thinking, and never do?

Punish my soul – supply my dreams.

We write a test each and every day and find out the answers later, though never knowing for which question.

She is a sham – a trick – a new ghost – a good girl that isn't. Where the ~~fuck~~ is the story if she was just a good girl.

A woman set for seduction, a woman set for tears, a woman set for my bitter worst. I will break her heart. I will have her husband a drunk. I will have her children on medication I will have their grandparents suffer for all they've given.

At first though I will be her happiness – everyone will see her glow – all her family impressed!

I think she is being strangled by life and has no way out so I'll offer her some relief–love, and ask no questions.

A normal woman a normal family – why is normal the greatest attraction? That is not what a love story should be.

Neha is saving for a trip to South Asia.

After two weeks I'm touching Neha like she talked of touching, kind.

6

EUPHORIA – WAS IT CHOPIN'S Nocturnal or Beethoven Silenco? I can't say I listened to them both completely – like afternoon high tea, except I was at complete peace, no tea. It wasn't the sonata's trance, it was that I was well enough to choose them to listen.

The next day, the same.

The happiest I could be.

And the next day again.

Three days was enough.

By the fourth day I was searching for euphoria and thus my mistake.

You can be happy, you can be grouchy – you can be what you like – if it is productive at that juncture in space. But you can't have the same feeling everyday as then the feeling would never exist, you'd just be.

This is true of everything in life – the best drinker, the worst drunk, the best lover, the worst spouse.

We are all happy obnoxious when at the best and completely need to laugh when we are the worst.

Neha thinks she has the recipe.

Veronica and I would fight, argue mostly. You tend to leave out the eighty percent non-communicating and reference the twenty percent harmony.

It has been silly, my thoughts of Veronica, a woman of her age and a man of my age may sound bizarre to a young adult – I'll tell you some thoughts never change, just perception changes.

I was on a losing streak when I was introduced to Veronica and I was susceptible to making a mistake for sex. I could fall for false love, I could be caught without caution going through three red lights – ruin my life.

Except things have changed... I have experience, I have a wife.

As complicated as can be.

What kind of kindness did Veronica speak of?

Neha sweet, 'Kind like you make me feel now. I can keep this kindness all day. And you can too.'

True, I hold at the edge of man the entire day and clear my mind of stress looking for her to come again. There is no finish, there is no start – no frustration because we are so happy this way. Weeks of bliss, a height of near ecstasy without ever finishing – except we do, I do, she must. 'You help me release all my stress of the day.' Her words I have never heard someone say with so much flawless perfume. 'I'm not easy to live with, you aren't missing anything, can promise you.'

Maybe I'm too old. I'm too old.

I have thoughts of impossible with Neha.

I married my wife because she never questioned – she gave me tea in my locked room; she understood I need to write. They all say 'write' but when they live with it they can't stand it, they can't handle it. If you cut wood, build a car, it is easy, it can be seen. Words on paper, thinking in the mind, they don't understand.

Now my wife has seen me writing for a lifetime and nothing, no money, she says, 'Write, but money too.' She must wonder why I continue to waste my time.

And what would Neha say if I spent all day at my desk between Internet and reading – walk, exercise, write, play soccer with my son?

She would say nothing if money comes – they all say nothing if money comes.

I have no intention of going to work, ever.

Neha and I didn't even laugh at first. It wasn't until we freshened up that we laughed and thought it was okay that we hadn't broken a barrier – we'd just sampled fruit.

'I always knew I could trust you,' she says as I step out of the door. 'The truth is, I probably wouldn't have stopped you.'

It is a paradox, isn't it? I let you because I trust you and at the same time if you do cross the line I wouldn't let you. Do what you do to me – what feels so good to me – is also what stops you.

I think run away with her – jump in the pool with her, destroy my life, destroy hers. I have no means to take care of her.

I don't ask her about home life – I will never ask her about home life. Veronica says Neha is happy with home life and I believe her.

—

As little as Neha talks – I listen.

Now take off your clothing so we can make poetry – no that wouldn't be interesting, keep your clothing on, we will do everything but we don't, we don't do anything = poetry = I'm no writer.

Please manipulate me, tarnish my reputation, sabotage my mind. Make me broke for scent. I'll eat and eat and walk away. You'll like that. I won't bother you and then you'll remember, send me a polite nothing – close it. We can't marry; we're married.

I know her voice is different when she addresses others. Her aroma is clean, romantic, friendly, harmless, laughing at my comments, commenting on my clothing, smirking when we talk. She learns how I eat, what I drink – she loves something about me.

I wasn't overly aroused or shaking, sweating, or full of sexual attack. It was just a massage – natural – taking care of man. A haunting as this I must take my turn. Instead she rises up before I can flourish her with touches of joy. I'm left for the first time with some kind of rejection, some kind of let down – something in the air, some kind of dynamic is to change up or down I don't know, but our ability to sustain is now shaken. We cannot go on for ever incitement.

'I have to go home,' she says.

I understand. I'm not a hundred percent – a magnet does not pull me – I'm enjoying. She is not a hundred percent for me too.

—

Neha sees me immediately this morning as soon as Veronica leaves the house.

'The truth – you really want the truth – the truth is: no. Nothing will happen, you are much older than me and that is speaking as if we were both single. You see, even if I was alone and you were alone it still, it still couldn't be. We are what and all we can be.'

I don't speak.

'I shouldn't have spoken,' she ends.

Slow – we cool each day. I see her polite smiles or hello – nothing more, until today. We work together near noon – now in my room for tea. She has her home made lunch, she shares fruit.

Lunch is over, she gets up to leave. I don't move. I just sit on the sofa as she walks out.

All entertainment – none of this is life until it crosses into my family and bank account.

Perfect at this junction.

—

Mushrooms mixed with cocaine can give you the perceived ability to hear words from others minds. Words that aren't spoken, only thought through a silent mouth. Telepathy, I don't know.

Cocaine alone dangerous – mushrooms alone, frightening – together, control.

I jumped in twenty-five years ago, invested into Tru's business. Celebrate.

Alone, downstairs in Tru's basement with his sometimes girlfriend, blonde, smart, lost kind, she was never on my radar, polite and nothing more – I laughed, as it wouldn't be a relationship, they'd date and separate. I've never thought of her passionately until we tripped on mushrooms fueled by free base cocaine.

I read her mind.

Her mind spoke a humanly demanding, impressively clear sentence: 'Make love to me,' after an enjoyable hit.

We began to kiss hastily – enlightened, clothes off.

Tru was somewhere upstairs with his friends. Soon though Tru walked downstairs and saw us actively naked, engaged.

He glimpsed, turned closed the door and walked back upstairs – we continued to read minds ~~make love.~~

I don't know if he saw her again. I didn't see her again.

Wasn't long before my money was gone stolen, lost – Tru refused to accept responsibility, dismissing my claim. Charged forty minutes with his sometimes girlfriend instead of a black eye. Tru said, 'I told you. You can reinvest, go into business with us and make three times the money you'd lost. Quit complaining about your money, look at the good time you had.'

Tru's argument was that I received, cocaine, mushrooms, and his girlfriend as compensation.

I simply borrowed some money back from him – what comes around goes around as they say and never paid him back.

You never sign a contract with Tru – if you lose the money you have no recourse but to invest again and recoup. I wasn't a long-time investor.

I waited through-threating messages.

I didn't kill him, is what I'd intended to do.

Tru's rip off of my funds forgot, but never done again. Easy come easy go is a great catch phrase.

He knew I was to cheat him – he could live with it. If I cheated him he'd have another chance at my dependence on him. This is what he's after, full investment till you can't get out. This is the mind of Tru – score now, worry about the details later.

I shouldn't have made love with her. I shouldn't have read her mind. I shouldn't have done mushrooms with cocaine. I never should have invested money with Tru.

I've done all of these things – what did I learn?

I learned, minds can be read. Really, is this what I learned?

After time, Tru picked me up, took me for a drive in his car. I thought maybe he was going to try and knock me out, tempt me with a knife or something like that – he was that sort of guy – you were in or you were out.

First thing he did was park the car and lay out heroin to snort.

I'm thinking maybe friend, maybe not.

I'm no expert, but after I snorted the heroin my thoughts calmed, and the drive proceeded.

I studied telephone lines and electrical wires as he drove and made collections.

The song, 'I fought the law', a rendition by The Clash was playing on the radio. I'm a fan of The Clash, but not this particular song.

Tru abruptly turned off the radio when he heard the line 'I fought the law and the law won'.

A little more heroin, and all was forgot.

I ask Machine, why do I have to tell such stories?

If everything you do is good, what can you learn? Machine asks.

I can learn from others that do wrong.

Experience is the truest form of understanding. But you do not need to learn everything; some things aren't meant to be experienced.

Are you ill or clever? Machine asks.

Fire has been burning in me – fire to be good.

Machine says, 'If you are going to pretend to be good then what good are you?'

Good is depending – the corrupt are followed too.

The most wonderful time, the most wonderful favor – dimensions. How you get to a place of peace, a place of fear, is many scenes construed.

Diamond.

Now I sit thinking maybe business with Tru.

We are still friends, friends for thirty-two years.

It will not be a simple thing as putting money down and wait for investment to rise or fall, or be paid for my hours of labor – it will be life altering. I will never be the same again.

Machine says, 'Like many people, you've walked on water, you have read minds, you've received messages from above, within, you've foreseen the future, you have flown in the past, you've been close to death and seen the light calling you back to life. You've done what the prophets of popular culture have done except the prophets marketed, the greatest communicators spelled it in astounding words – magical sentences, skilled paragraphs expanding the readers direction to heavenly sentiment.'

I say, Machine you are wrong = the Prophets writers made it difficult to relate like many numbers not understood, if you can't add up the numbers it must be intelligent, if you can't understand sentences it must be important. To not make sense is grand smart – simple is to understand, can be challenged.

You can't challenge what you don't understand, especially when it doesn't make sense. Take those good books and tell me what they say. They all say argue everyday – game – they confuse – vague – stories they can twist if challenged, change if found out. They adapt to what is found, weak to strength with an altered importance.

Grand smart.

Like a lover you keep going back to because you don't understand. A true lover tells you, spells it in simple terms. A true lover comes through day after day.

The lover you chance is hit and miss, playing games... you love them or do you love the complication of figures of amusement of challenge? Take God Idol Deity, give it an explanation – the greatest lover ever – you can't lock up you can't depend...you beg and after a hundred times It appears once when you need It most, or It appears many times until you need It now and It is gone, no-where to be found?

A lover who wants you for selfish reasons will paint the greenest pasture, and say there, can't you see it?

A lover who is in love and nothing else will speak of hope of green pastures – they can't produce it, they can't fake it, because together you must make it.

The pain you feel is steady – live with imperfection.

Gives you something to do.

Miracles, super powers, spiritual texts – debunking them, relating to them, understanding them, recreating them, we are all prophets, we are all daughters and sons of gods – we are all messengers, we are all spirits but someone has to be king ape if you want to take the job.

We can be friends with everyone and we should be kind and friendly to all, but I will warn you, if you have heard stories of one who has cheated they may have cheated more than once and if they have developed a habit – even you a friend – the habit will trump and sometime, someday, you may never even know they cheat you. The cheat can save your live one day and cheat you out of life the next day. This is why they are so romantic – so story told – loved and hated: save you from being tied to the railway tracks then throw you out of an airplane. Sounds just like God to me – so go ahead and worship, go head and try and make sense of the verses you read.

When God lets you down he says devil – like the cheat he'll never admit it was he or she, they'll say it was someone else. When it serves the cheat right they'll admit the truth – at least they admit. God never admits – just keeps saying hell, devil, or you have done wrong.

I was to visit Tru – a simple thought of doing business may have been an answer of yes before I had children – chance and excitement has left my plate.

Keep my name safe.

I will skip Tru.

7

NO WORD IN ENGLISH can describe my wife – the rest of the world is black and white. I knew my wife wasn't real the first time I hugged and kissed her. She was hollow inside. Everything seemed real on the outside but inside she's only a spirit. She'll kill love dead, put me out of my misery, let me forget about love for all time, ~~and just fuck.~~

I felt my wife's spirit three meters away – maybe I felt her energy twelve thousand kilometers away.

I thought to walk away, prove ruler but my wife followed and pushed me – you haven't choice when you're dealing with a person whom is a spirit inside.

I wasn't afraid. I welcomed it.

It would be nothing for her to gut a person physically with a knife, or mentally with the same result.

An example: – a woman was being unpleasant with my wife and my wife said to her, 'Be nice to me, or you'll have a problem. Not a problem from me, but a problem from spirits of the dead.'

My children tell me I'm scared of Mom.

They're wrong, I'm never scared of her – I'm experimenting in another dimension. I like the control over a living spirit. I'm human so to speak. A normal human would never like to last with my wife, and vice versa.

What inhabits her? I don't know – I'm taught the fool, I'm taught love, I'm taught humble. I'm taught everything that I thought I'd passed – when you raise children, when you have a wife, all your weaknesses become abruptly upfront. What you think, what you struggle – after tears, after near violence, holler, yell, then peace... all becomes clear – a lesson taught, learnt.

I'm standing, asking what the next lesson is, she provided me Buddha. Buddha a vehicle for a much more advanced system – the system is alive as the wind the trees.

We are building the human until we are looking at ourselves – the clone, the clone is nothing – to look into ourselves, to build ourselves, to understand every thought, reason of our self's every mistake understood every stake of fame understood is something.

Clone is copied, it isn't built.

You will build yourself. Feel it, think it.

When you choose a mate, it isn't just you.

You wonder why?

You question what you feel?

What you feel is stronger than what you may want. What you feel becomes what you want.

Vice versa, what you want becomes not what you feel.

The most imperfect carbon-based machine that ever survived.

The hidden mind, you have to watch where you go.

Veronica and I both accepted it as pleasure and thus nobody hurt, only learnt. No money. No contract. No guarantee, and no insurance. We were exclusive together in a world of our own with no rules, creative to each other, unseen by others.

The human lie machine, it works.

A good meal is what most hope.

Take what is yours graciously as a gift and you'll feel well – take more and you'll feel bloated.

Here I am today benefiting from the pleasure of the time I'd spent with Veronica – it all turns around they say; spend the time and it will spend back on you someday.

Laka Wapa always waits.

Haunting has no essence of time – it is inconsiderate. Have fun figuring out which pleasures you are answering for.

Haunting Warnings! = Gut, nature, instinct, and the unknown.

Killing – burning inside.

Haunting laughing and you wonder who: an associate, a close friend, distant relative, spirits, ha ha ha devil gods, karma, cause and effect, ocean of life, stars moon sun, universe, asteroid, alien, or none of them.

How about you? Fungus, molecule, organic, the government, the secret police, the computer, the hack, or perhaps poisoned brain.

Yelling, screaming my wife's name out at night. I knew how cause and effect worked and I knew the skill my future wife held, I knew my sensitivity, a one-woman man. I drove to Veronica's home before I made the final commitment to be with my wife.

Veronica, yogi wide – barbarian – in shape, benching the barrier, devilish, no longer defender, playmaker!

I knew where my mind was at. I knew where my head was at. Friends. Let lose – human I am. Steal my soul. I above she below, mean friend swallow me whole – consume me – lust, sex, intercourse was filling the room as close to naked breach as two can be.

I slipped away, vanished the night, drove my car insane, nearly cry. I didn't want to lose my future Cambodian wife.

Veronica lay naked, silent, annoyed I don't know – understanding I don't know – pregnant? No.

I never returned to see Veronica. We caught each other at the shopping mall at the service station, waved on the road.

—

I talk a lot, but I don't know the recipe.

Love is imperfect.

Lose all your money in complete contempt, still love. Split the front lip, still love, burden of another child, still love – don't get mixed up in it. I'm telling you. A habit you'd once quit, still love.

And yet I don't need it – I don't need love.

I find love because it is expected of me. I'm expected to find something as dreadful as love.

Once tasted, I can't chase it away. For some reason my body loves the pain, loves the pulse beat – the heat, the heel to neck spinning top.

Before Veronica, before my wife, a Venezuelan panther of ivory skin solved love and sex – I realized the color of soul with her... the same as my wife.

Veronica was only water between coke and brown sugar.

Broke, desperate, rich – poetry.

Travel alone – no use for good.

I've never been able to get this Venezuelan Panther out of my head, an intrigue I refuse to forget.

For myself she had a perfect aura.

Not a crush – a magnificent sequence.

I knew a relationship was impossible, a pregnancy plausible.

Like a shooting star, bright brilliant and then

I was gone from Venezuela.

No address, no phone number. In time I forgot her last name. She hasn't faded, only stronger in my mind. How ridiculous is that? Just two-pieces of meat that wrapped around my prick became a spirit haunting me.

This is the heartbreak that is made by myth, that you travel back to in your mind – different than having your heart broken. A broken heart I can't talk about because I never experienced it. I experienced the best time.

You can always find love the social way, the Internet. The slow honest way like we fall in love with a classmate, a work mate, a selection from a calendar, a match making, like how we fall in love with someone we've been around, like the love for a flower, a stray cat is the safer bet. Researched, tried. Stable. But what will you do when you see the aura, the sparkle in the eye that takes you to the stars? An explosion ending all other humans because only you and her matter. Stars and explosions are violent, cruel, and when the eruption is done you have life or death. There is always a consequence. It may be calm, it may be empty.

I can describe it, the human color that you'll see or have seen – all the cells in your body will celebrate glory, they'll thrive in the emotion of grandeur too bleak.

This illumination called – well I can't call it love because you can love anything, I'll call her 'Universe'. I don't even have to look; she'll find me just like the Venezuelan Panther, put me through the grinds, jump through the hoops until desolate rock bottom down she'll have me and I'll be caught, and then I'll return the favor and bring her to misery until we are even – a deal can be struck, a universe created. My deal with the Panther was never to see her again. With my wife it will be...well, you figure it out.

Making love is something, leaving this earth naked out to the universe and back again is another.

Why do I think of a woman so far away, so far gone in time? I think of her to satisfy, to get a kick. Small kicks of pleasure, all I have to do is remember our time together, further inoculating the drug.

I'm doing it right now, writing this down, thinking of her – even though I know I'll never ever see her again.

Addict.

Now my wife, chaotic Khmer, she walked into a restaurant and I didn't fall down – I traveled in space above the ground towards her, reminiscent of Venezuela.

Unexpectedly life altering – all those dreams, all those disappointments of love – stabbed, scorched, follow what earthly says, do no more.

I knew as soon as we made love. I didn't care if she got pregnant. I wanted her pregnant. She was vying like the rest of the cultures to subdue my blood in her kind. I let my semen enter, the fish swam and I selected to mix two cultures and become one – a gift, a child with her.

I never thought twenty years. I thought two years and a baby, that is all.

Why should I write a tragic love story when I can live one?

Don't have a wife who wants to be happy.

Have a wife who wants you happy and if you do the same, so be happy – but never content, if content, then what?

My wife knowingly loves to interrupt my thoughts.

'Where are you today? Are you here? Or are you in there?'

'In there' meaning my brain.

I ask her, 'Where?'

'Where-ever you go when you hide inside your mind.'

The market, I play.

'If it's to the market that you go inside your head then it is better to stay at the market instead of back to some girl that you liked before. I know you like to think about some girl in South America you frigged before.'

It is true the South American spirit shone, the light projected the plane I reached for. Everything through the years, in-between her and my wife, lame practice, no darkness of universe where light is a lover of colossal energy un-held by spinning earth.

If you have experience, you can find an attractive woman, a desirable woman, smart, educated, caring, respectable – a woman many men would love to marry, a woman you could hold hard for hours and still, if she is not a dangerous stranger from an outer world you will continue to search.

If you haven't met this experience then it doesn't matter you relate to a different experience – maybe my experience is the evil spirit.

Who knows!

A junky only understands a junky.

For I, the experience, matters over all else.

A love story I could write forever because there is no such thing and being no such thing, it is infinity – it will never stop, love will never stop.

I've tried as hard as I can, not to write about her. As hard as the man who says he no longer believes in faith but ask it daily in trauma.

—

Ivory

I tell everyone that love will come and you will know it.

I've told my wife about her and my wife wonders why I left her or she left me. My wife doesn't understand it was only to be as it was. It was the edge of crazy with life trying to be lived all at once, and then over. What can I tell you – sex, love, jealousy, infatuation, exaggeration, first love, confusion, distrust, angst, utter dizziness; it was never to be a commitment, that is why it has become so unique. It was unwilling to compromise, unable to be. Torture – a hungry thirst that needed to be.

I'd just turned twenty years old.

Soap operas and variety shows are quite good in Venezuela. Good television, lots of hot water, modern facilities, clean, and a decent color scheme; my room at the Clarion Hotel in Caracas. By timing or by guides, I felt right at the Clarion. To go back in the past is dreadful, as I tell this story I haven't a mind or heart, because the past is now gone. Yet upon finding the Clarion hotel and onward is an astounding phase in my life.

In my slouching way I turned my head towards the entrance of the Clarion hotel lounge as I sat in the lobby, and there she was walking past me towards the lounge, her long black hair shining, not even a glance my way. How many chances may I have? I'd danced with her in a disco a month earlier though nothing transpired. I'd been waiting to find her again. It's something you knew would happen. I never knew I'd find her at the Clarion hotel lounge where I drank or ate every other day, but I'd find her somewhere. She started working in the lounge that evening. It was to be when a woman shines as a star in a grey backdrop.

Red lips, full voluptuous red.

Not at all tall, far from petite, fair Latin skin, and straight, sensual, l thick black hair that was longer than her back and quit at her bottom. When she spoke, I understood. Her Spanish came to me like English. I didn't see other women – slow, I'd visit her with plans of the future.

Her phone number on polished paper.

I called.

Ivory turned me down.

I was not incensed, much worse than this.

A discovery.

I hurt.

Find another girl.

Two beers, no four, beers no ten beers, I never got that far, I never even got past one before I was intercepted by a pair of eyes and an unconscious mood. A woman had found me in a restaurant across the street from the hotel. I'd wandered in for a few beers to take back to my room.

Our eyes transfixed.

Blame Ivory for this.

I sat, as the woman finished her meal – sure she'd seduced me and I responded, unaware of fear – I had been hurt and now I didn't care what, most days I'd be afraid and shy away.

The woman claimed she was a dancer, twenty-nine years of age.

A long body, tanned skin, dancer legs, I jumped in. It didn't take much to clear misery, a perfect night that extended through the next day and another night.

I don't know why she stayed with me a second night.

Maybe it was I the first night, and cocaine the next day.

By morning two, sober reality. I'd seen enough of her.

She suggested we meet at the beach, I disagreed. I was on my way – destiny.

But not so sure – it would take another event before I could swallow all of Ivory's heart.

Ivory knew about the dancer.

I sat down beside Ivory expecting some sort of jealous response – embarrassed I think, I smirked. She answered much better than with sadness or rage. She surprised me when she said she'd seen me holding hands with the dancer. This wasn't the only surprise.

Ivory smiled and spoke,

'Now you can be my boyfriend.'

I didn't believe her. She confessed we'd go out – still maybe it wouldn't be true.

We went out, held hands, ate, danced, embraced, laughed, and kissed.

A problem arose on our second date after much romance, caressing, and drink. She came back to the Clarion hotel only to be stopped at the reception desk. She wasn't allowed up to my room because she worked in the Clarion lounge. We said good night.

Ivory was taking it slow, incensing me.

I could escape frustration with a trip out of town – disappear – break her nonexistent heart, instead of a painful wait.

My friend Madoc owed me an investment.

To collect I'd have to leave the city.

This is the second event that would lead to my broken heart. And just in time my nerves were almost to burst as I was on schedule to do something stupid and lose a chance with Ivory forever.

If you want a woman, walk away. If you don't want her whole, don't leave and let her have her way with you. If you can't handle all of her, leave and never come back.

I left the Clarion hotel without notice.

—

Madoc (Mad Doctor) a forty-two-year-old kid.

He came from Guyana, his ancestors from India.

I'd lived with Madoc for a few months before I moved into the Clarion Hotel so I knew him well enough to trust.

He'd lived in Venezuela for many years, speaking a language of his own, a mixture of British, Caribbean, and American with mumbled chants and roars. I couldn't understand his Spanish and I couldn't understand his English, I wonder if the people of his homeland understood him?

As a man once put it, 'Nobody understands Madoc.' Madoc spoke with the exuberance of a man leaping off a ledge, happily. A short man with a likeable face, somewhat athletic, he claimed to be an expert swimmer. He didn't have expensive clothing but he did well in the dress pants, shirts, and suits he wore.

He asked if I snow skied – I certainly have and I certainly did.

We'd spend four days a week on snow (cocaine).

Madoc was a fiend, a con, a laugh, a casualty, and also a friend. If I was asked the question, 'Have you ever recognized an unfamiliar face?' I'd say 'yes' and it would be this man from behind the reception desk. This is how I saw Madoc my first night in Caracas, behind a hotel reception desk, smiling. That first night in South America he had me seeing the walls in my hotel room grow large, while the room grew small.

He ambushed me a few evenings later, claiming he's a visionary with hints that he could read my past. I speculated, for I figured it was all common sense to guess one's past. I implored him to scan my past and infiltrate my future. The nerve of him attempting to serve out my history, my worries, my nightmares, and my future fortune, indeed I loved it. He started with my family and then proceeded to a tree. Imagine Madoc at his best reading, with my encouragement he discovered a tree, ha, ha, ha. Yes, a tree.

The Mad-Doctor's words, 'There was a tree close to your home when you were growing up, it was very special to you, you'd pass it on your way to school.'

I almost laughed – a tree.

Don't we all have trees? After all, I was raised in Canada. But I have no special tree, secure branch, or keepsake leaf.

I smiled at him and answered, 'Yes, there was a tree.'

Many trees evoked, but none of which were strong enough to change a life or love. I said, 'Yes, there was a tree,' to keep him searching for more. He continued and I kept saying yes.

The truth being, ever since the day of the tree reading, trees have become an intricate part of my life. The prominent, large, lonely tree is the best. They exhale great strength and I grasp their power to heal, meditate. Had he planted this in my mind or have I acquired a taste for trees on my own? A little suggestive thought may grow.

When Madoc first came to Venezuela, he lived in the mountains and fished the rivers for food. He lived on a combination of fish, fruit, and vegetables, all free, from Mother Earth. He slept under a thousand stars, sold fruit and fish for money. I know he was in the military, but never liked it. He made himself a life, raising a family, a wife and a daughter. The raising family part long since ended as far as I could see. He talks much about his daughter, this is where a large portion of his money goes. Still, time is invaluable.

Although the hotel reception jobs never paid all that well, the added bonus of socializing with tourists helped inflate his wage, depending on how he socialized. He was always making deals with the tourists, he could find them anything they wanted and not always for a price. Madoc did a lot of favors without kickback. His weakness was the American and European beauty. The extra money he made off tourists he usually spent with tourists. Madoc was a complicated man. He'd look for deficiencies. Like a therapist he would try to solve his problems. I think he liked the constant fuck-ups in his life. He had the read on people from his own mistakes. Madoc was a practitioner, discovering the painful issues of others by using his own history as clues. Madoc liked to point out the hidden, comforting himself with the notion he was not alone in the stark schedule of days to nights.

Living with Madoc was defying all that most people believe as a good vacation or trip. I cared nothing of the fantasy vacation. The back packers, the resort lizards, the tourists, the jet setters, they had nothing on me. Wisdom and mythical powers were an everyday occurrence, a scholar taking notes.

We didn't travel far, down to the all-day cinema, Hong Kong fight movies or the European pornographic flicks. I'd sleep or meditate during the fight films and wonder why everyone reads a newspaper before the start of the porno movies. Madoc danced and sung-song in the room, dances of the seventies disco era and folk songs of his homeland. I waited on money and drugs as Madoc devoured my mind.

'You can be invisible, you can stop time. You can have protection from above.' These words impacted me. I believed him. With much discussion I solidified exactly how to become invisible. Confidence, days and weeks of unbridled thought, focused on one symbol, invisible, conquest and walk. In the end they still see you, but their mind doesn't click in the reference, they transfer your image to another part of their brain, a notation isn't taken, you're not stopped, you're not questioned. You've sent a message, don't record, I'm invisible. You just don't register.

I left the Clarion hotel unannounced to go on an adventure with Madoc.

The sun, the moon, you have it every day so I shouldn't have to describe the sky at all in this story, you know it's hot most times, rains sometimes, and is cold once in a while. Wind, and humidity you know that too. My skin burns, I burn bad, blonde hair and fair skin. I consider myself pleasant to look at and peculiar in actions and speech.

I was to meet Madoc on the street and we were to go to the sea.

Causally I walked down the street, luggage in hand – Madoc couldn't pick me up at the Clarion; he was highly suspicious.

A gleaming four-door sedan pulled up, a taxi. Bags in the trunk, I'm in the back-seat, Madoc in the front with the driver who had a weakness for Madoc's sordid antics. The driver smoked tobacco stacked with freebase cocaine while driving us out of the city to the coast.

The drive was anything but splendid – Madoc freebased-up, a glowing sight, I too sulking Ivory. Madoc though displayed dramatics, theatrical productions to thwart being followed.

I thought of Ivory full force, pounding, aching, oozing so far from dirty, so far from erotic, just lovely Ivory the being. Ivory surrounded with every word I spoke and with every word I'd heard, all reflections Ivory. She said she would be my girlfriend, that I'd heard. We'd dated. We hadn't articulated. This is what I waited, this is for what I longed, Ivory bled on my cock, carved on my back.

When we reached the coast, Madoc spoke candidly, 'If I die, contact my mother, give her this paper.' The paper contained a hastily written will and testament, scribbled down during the early morning on a sleepless night. In any event he left for the city or somewhere.

With no beer, no cocaine, no food, not to mention little sleep for days, I began twitching from head to toe. My body became an entity of its own, convulsing.

My leg popped. My hand reached for the leg and my arm quivered in succession until my entire body twirled in the air, snapping and contracting. I was bouncing a foot off the bed, an acrobat. Trusting the next jerk won't be a dead jerk.

I did find the trick to sanity, it was to never move my head, and my body wouldn't twitch. If I stayed still, I'd survive, if I moved I'd be dead.

I spent a day and a night in seclusion. Wait, I did have a visitor, the hotel receptionist. She knocked at the door looking for money. I knew I couldn't move or answer the door. I had the correct amount of money in the front pocket of my jeans. The jeans I was wearing. Unable to move my head, let alone get up and answer the door I told her to use her key and come in. Even in my desperate condition I still wanted to fuck her. She was young and attractive. I blew that though. She strained at the sight of me, like I was some kind of a freak. And freak I did when I put my hand in my front pocket. I lifted my head ever so slightly and that did it. Never lift your head when you're twitching. I managed to get the money out of my pocket while I quivered onto my side. My body was out of control. I bounced onto my stomach and then on to my other side, a complete rotation. One rotation wasn't enough, my body quivered, twisted, and bounced around a second time as I delivered the money in mid-air to her hand, so funny yet most tragic. The receptionist petrified. I'm surprised she hadn't phoned a doctor for me.

The next day the manager asked us to leave. He said we weren't the right kind of customers for the hotel.

Madoc returned, shoved cocaine into my nostril, gave me a free-based cocaine cigarette, a beer, and I was okay. I walked out of the hotel stumbling and stuttering – looking for a burger.

Burger boy and girl laughing as my language was scattered. What a good tasting burger it was on this day.

The next morning evicted from our hotel – no problem, Madoc booked us into a nicer place. After checking in, we went to a resort hotel on the beach where a safety deposit box was in Madoc's name. Although Madoc didn't have the key, the key was in the possession of a German who didn't want Madoc to access the safety deposit box. The German didn't want his own name on the box – he forgot how brazen Madoc was or didn't care.

At the reception desk, Madoc showed his identification and explained how he'd lost the key. The hotel called in maintenance promptly. With a drill in hand, maintenance drilled a hole and took out the lock. Inside was a folder envelope bursting full. Madoc handed me the thick envelope folder and we walked out to the street. We walked a distance to find a taxi and then our hotel room. Madoc opened the envelope and took out the package inside, he divided the cocaine, filled package in half, half kilo for me, half kilo for him.

After an hour I slipped out of the hotel room to cool down and have a drink at the pool-side lounge.

A woman sat next to me, she was acquainted with the barmaid. Sometimes you speak and present yourself and on this day I spoke in depth. I got personal. My situation with immigration was put on the table. I'd been staying in Venezuela without the proper paper work – an expired visa. The woman seated next to me was full of solutions. Just look what happens when you open up to a stranger? You receive sympathetic gifts.

Her first consideration, 'If you're short of money, you can stay at my beach house.' Her English was impeccable. 'My parents are in the government, I can get you the papers to stay here as long as you like.'

Suddenly the visa she could grant me was secondary to living at her beach house.

We'd date this night, she was thirty-four years old and far from sexy, she certainly wasn't cute. I felt that she was going to buy me, the exchange of flesh for favors. I must go out with her immediately.

I showered, dressed, and made my way for my date, there wasn't a decision to be made. I would attend to the rich. She was in the lobby on time, and looking well, good actually.

We drove from the sea back to the city. Like I'd been exiled and tonight I was sneaking back unnoticed. She drove one of those expensive all-terrain vehicles. The fashionable expensive district was where she parked her truck. On the trip in she explained how she intended to buy a nightclub and that's where we were going. She chatted up the owner, while I ate and drank, a rather good time as I didn't have to speak. Only perform at a motel.

It started off fine, dirty talk, exaggerated lust. She ripped her shirt, undid her skirt, naked her and I. I thought she was going to hyperventilate when we started fucking. Would I have to call a nurse?

She pushed me over mid-seduction.

I tried to slow her down.

She gained an edge of energy and toppled me. Her eyes crazy, her hair in disarray, her body moaning, gyrating, and my voice lost. 'Slow down,' I wanted to shout.

She was so excited, screaming away, fucking her brains out. I wanted nothing of it. I was going down, I was growing soft, I wanted her off. With all my strength I threw her off.

I stood and shouted, 'What are you doing? You could get a disease.'

I had to say something, some sort of compensation for my inability.

My worst performances are always the ones I least care to engage. I didn't apologize, I dressed. I remember nothing once in her truck. I passed out. I woke up with her screaming, 'You could have had anything you wanted, anything.' If I'd just slept with her.

I never answered.

Silence.

She dropped me at my hotel.

I couldn't fuck the rich.

Today I think I should have. I'd be living at her beach house screwing a young sultry colored girl when the rich woman was away, the good life. I'm really stupid, it would have been perfect, my papers in order and to hell with scams. Just swim, run, read, write, stroll the cafes and fuck for money until I met some good looking rich girl who finds herself pregnant, we'd be married, divorced, and I'd be set for life. What a nice story. It wasn't to be – Ivory!

—

After a day of rest, I took a taxi into Caracas, my choices were to stay near the ocean or move to the city. Ivory won, I moved in two blocks from the Clarion Hotel. Ivory – I wanted to hurt her. I wanted to stay away but the atmosphere of the Clarion hotel beckoned.

Hugs and smiles, questions, and joy, Ivory brilliant. A wild mood caught me.

Ivory invited herself, or I invited her back to my room.

She listened as I spoke in Spanish and swore in English. I had this incredible woman lounged out on my bed and I released my frustration. Not once did I consider her, must have been love.

After several hours, Ivory exhausted from listening to my rant on life, went home.

True, I'd been taking too much drug and drink.

True, she wasn't completely sober, though not on the same stratosphere as me.

The next night the roles reversed, she talked all night, snorting cocaine and I just listened, thinking I'll never be with her.

I'd talked her ear off and she'd talked my ear off, nothing romantic. I'd conceded defeat, we were friends. Nothing is worse than friends.

I'd forfeited any sexual attempts with Ivory, maybe that's why I felt so normal. I'd stayed away from the Clarion for a couple of days until Ivory phoned.

She suggested we go out.

It felt more like a chore than an event.

Up the stairs we went to my room after drinks and dinner.

Ivory walked the stairs behind me, pinched my bottom once, then twice.

She said, 'Tonight, I don't want talk, I want sex.'

Dizzy – so intense I can't fathom.

They say, float on air.

Stars, explosions, all true, who wrote this, knew love.

We staggered forwards, backwards, sideways.

Unable to unlock my hotel room door, we fell to the floor of the hall. We managed to compose ourselves long enough to put the key in properly and enter my room. This is when time slowed and silence prevailed, we undressed. She led me to a wooden chair against the wall. I sat, she turned her back to me. She lowered herself slowly onto the tip of my knob, moistly inching down.

Time is mystery.

She lifted up and turned her body to face me.

She straddled deeper down.

Adrenaline lifted.

Before I could digest the greeting, she rose, took my hand to the bathroom.

On top of the porcelain she stood, her legs slightly flexed.

My mind faint, I floated in a dimension unseen.

The porcelain is accented extreme plain white, cold, hard.

Truth.

On my tiptoes, I struggled to journey deep.

She squatted lower and I stretched. I expanded, I grew tall, went deep.

I looked in the mirror holding back romantic collapse. Beauty, I could see beauty.

I could have exploded but the trip was too lively. I'd stopped time, everything stood still. A silent film slowed in today's technology.

Enhancing my pulsating existence, I would not moan.

Peace in quiet.

She stood up and stepped down.

We floated to the bed as spirits, as one again.

Shocking motions still, my existence halted by her sight. A painting, a witch, a crazed woman from outer space, not animal or human, a super being, eyes which cried terror and for moments I heard no noise. She could see what I saw at the same moment. Two aliens greeting for the first time, applauding exhaustion at berth, albeit harmonic, curtains till death.

This was making love with Ivory.

She corralled darkness, sucked up spirit and splattered it on canvass, still life!

I never came, my orgasm attained a frozen delight, held and at no time released, a polar deep inside a beautiful marine.

When I did come, it continued, no beginnings, no ends.

Underachieved, insignificant, the words I tremble when another woman tries to please.

Ivory on that day captured me.

Her eyes will draw me through the universe.

I will die with those eyes.

Her translucent stare at me for all time.

—

Jealousy – if I'm in love, I'm jealous. I won't deny, control it, yes, at this time – I did and didn't have control. I did pretty well.

I never asked her if she had other lovers. She asked if she could invite a girlfriend to make love with us.

We went out, met up, ate, drank.

Her girlfriend and I never smiled, never caught each other's eye. Ivory would have us try.

They stood at my door, Ivory and her girlfriend.

I wasn't attracted to Ivory's girlfriend.

I thought they wanted my cocaine, not me, my excuse.

I spoke, 'No,' and asked her girlfriend to leave. She left, sad.

A mistake, I don't know.

Ivory stayed.

This was my jealous time – another woman made me jealous because I never liked the other woman, simple as that.

When did my love flutter with Ivory? It was on a fine leather chair enjoying a cigarette in a cocaine moment in the lobby of the hotel. I was perfect. A man can look days for a few minutes of harmony. I wasn't going to waste the moment. I sat in astounding joy. She begged me to go upstairs to my room and I sat smiling, I wasn't listening, I wasn't moving, I was lost in my dream. She begged and the more she begged, the more I smirked. Ivory broke into a sob and ran out. The woman behind the reception scolded that I'd been awful, I trusted this woman's judgment and I chased after Ivory. When I caught up with her, she was bawling uncontrollable. I'd made a blunder. She wasn't coming back to my room, ever. Ever is a mighty long time. In a couple of nights Ivory was at my door; we made love like never before and never again. We didn't separate this night we made love all night, incredible love, exhausting love. The bliss I received after making intense love was attained and held several times without stopping – it was to hold the feeling of wealth after sex while still being slow in having sex. Cocaine lay on my cock, on her breasts, on her thighs. It was ten in the morning and we hadn't slept when Ivory came from the bathroom as white as a ghost. She was on the verge of fainting. I steadied her. Walked her to the street and hailed a taxi. When Ivory stepped toward the taxi she dropped to the pavement, exhausted. She spent the day in the hospital.

After this incident Ivory would phone my room in the afternoon only to listen, no hello, nothing, only silence.

I knew it was Ivory because she had to speak to the receptionist to get through to my room. She did this often. I seldom phoned her, or should I say I never phoned her. I lost her phone number somewhere. Our relationship was troubled yet neither of us refused to give up the torrid treacherous affair.

It wasn't all-good at the hotel – I let things slip, my own security was at risk.

I'd become careless in love.

I was also in trouble with hotel management who at the time I thought I could trust.

I joked much with the hotel staff and them with me but I was often late or behind on paying the hotel bill; even though I had enough money in cocaine to pay for many months, I didn't always have cash. One time, Ivory drew my cock on a piece of paper. I'd left the drawing of my cock on the night-stand and had forgotten about it. House cleaning got a hold of the famous cock. They paraded the drawing through the hotel, a big laugh. Part of my problem was drinking – the staff and manager became increasingly alarmed at my lack of eating and abundance of drinking. I'd begun a romantic association with hunger. I'd wait all day for a meal and project exactly how the ceremony would be held. Enticing how we revolve around a fuel called food. I loved the wait for a meal, the buildup to hunger. I was planning meals days in advance. It was an obsessive love affair that rivalled my thoughts of Ivory. And why shouldn't it? I could live without Ivory, but I couldn't live without food.

My body reeked of cocaine most mornings; my pores poured out archaic perfume. My temples wrapped in ice ached at night as I watched for the imaginary man on the rooftop across the street. Blood dribbled red from my nose to my bed sheet, my pillowcase served as my handkerchief. The smell, the stench disgusted Ivory, and the dirt on my feet between my toes horrified her. She'd pull me to the shower and clean me from head to toe, on her hands and knees scrubbing away, purifying my skin, my heart, my stark epilogue.

Ivory's sister entered the lounge and we chatted. Her sister was appealing, different than Ivory though, not as mysterious but a bit taller. Her sister did however speak English. Ivory was taking us out for drinks. She gave me strict orders to be on good behavior. We went to my room first so Ivory could freshen up. While Ivory was in the washroom I sat on the bed near her sister. I looked into her sister's eyes, she didn't resist, we embraced in a lovely kiss, tumbling back on the bed. A visibly upset Ivory caught us but said nothing. Her sister was embarrassed. Ivory rushed us out of the room. She did say something albeit, she had one request, don't drink brandy. When the waiter asked what I would like to drink, my answer was simple - Brandy. Ivory was furious. That was the end, Ivory dropped me off at the hotel; we were finished.

In two days the National Guard came to search my room.

House cleaning, concerned over my odd behavior, notified management on the blood splattered pillowcase and bed sheets each morning, not to mention I hadn't paid my hotel room bill for a week.

I'd given Madoc my cocaine a day earlier, sensing trouble was afoot. I told him it was better he stash it away, sell it or most likely do it, and then pay or reimburse me later. It was safer for him than I, as it did turn out. He'd always paid me back before.

The National Guard thought it was funny, they were asked to search and found nothing.

They did however find something, no visa in my passport.

My fast times had climaxed.

I was lucky not to have any drugs but unlucky to give them to a fiend.

I wasn't surprised I never saw Madoc again, though he was smart to ignore me.

I spent a couple of days in a military compound and then a few hours in an immigration cell. A man from Brazil, he could see my hunger, he gave me half his sandwich, a half cup of coffee, and two cigarettes while we sat together in immigration.

After a meeting with an immigration officer, good fortune, my passport still intact, free but an airplane flight must be booked to leave the country within seven days.

I would spend another five days in Caracas waiting for my flight. I slept on a couch in the hotel lobby for a couple of nights thanks to the night receptionist.

The Canadian Embassy coordinated a driver to take me to the airport, they also hand wrote a note in my passport stating that they'd seen my passport.

No phone numbers, no address exchange, no goodbye. It was a flagrant vacation, one I'd never do again yet not refuse.

I don't know if this time was an important moment or even a moment at all in Ivory, and Madoc's lives. They only met once for a brief introduction, seconds really. My time with them is a moment in my life – a moment I remember to share.

—

I was content I was going to write from an early age and thought it again and again.

I needed an example:

A biography on Henry Miller (author) and the movie Henry and June exposed much about Henry Miller's writing before I'd read a single word.

I ordered *Tropic of Cancer* and *Tropic of Capricorn*, already sure Miller was going to be important in my life.

Everything without editing.

Open any page and read.

Take a simple day and expand – didn't matter how wrenched his lovers could be as he could be just as sobering.

We all want to find our June, Henry's muse.

Live first and a story will come.

Henry Miller took his mind and put it on paper – the stories he read, the subjects he studied, his daily routine. He relayed his knowledge, right or wrong it was his knowledge on subjects – cultures, books, music, food, and sex.

After the *Tropic* books I wanted more from Henry Miller. I even read *Crazy Cock,* an unrefined work with a few exciting pages I'll never forget. T*he Rosy Crucifixion, Nexus, Plexus, Sexus,* confirmed my decision to follow him. I enjoyed *The Rosy Crucifixion* more than the *Tropic* books not because they were better but because I was reading Henry Miller day after day.

Henry was told, 'Write the way you talk.' He wrote the stories he told to the everyday person on the street, the brothel, the workplace. You wake up with him, go to a café, drink wine, and dream his dreams.

Over twenty years ago I'd picked up a list at the library of the 100 greatest fiction books. *Magus* by John Fowles (author) was on this list.

I ordered the revised version of the *Magus*.

The *Magus* changed everything about what a person could write. Finally, I read the complex thoughts of the human on paper in language I understood.

Yes *Magus* was the book to set me on my path – if Henry Miller is the artist, *Magus* is the book.

If Henry Miller is the author and *Magus* the book,

Paulo Coelho (author) is my grounding.

The Brazilian author of *The Alchemist* – some books stay with you for weeks, even months, and other books like *The Alchemist* will stay with you for life.

After reading *The Alchemist* I thought this must be a one off – never could an author repeat the feat. True maybe.

I chose his novel *Eleven Minutes* to read first after *The Alchemist* – as I didn't want to be disappointed. I wanted more of his thoughts. I liked him, and at least *Eleven Minutes* seemed rough, interesting, not a fairy tale. It is about a Brazilian prostitute in Europe.

I wasn't disappointed.

When reading Paulo Coelho, you know he isn't just writing from imagination, he is writing of experience. You listen to a story as told by the author as he travels, learns, and constructs it.

I was back to basics with Paulo Coelho, reminiscing thoughts I would never reveal, but believed.

Between reading Paulo Coelho's *Aleph* and *The Witch of Portobello*, I've been reading Charles Bukowski's *Women* and *Post Office*.

I laugh my head off – not at Bukowski – but at myself, the simplistic gaffes he's made me aware of. He's hilarious, especially at work – he can be the best employee or the worst. He is yin and yang and this is true of everything in his life.

Hank Bukowski is the straightforward character in his novels just like the author. What is the clear-cut way to write a novel? Write about your demanding or pleasurable day with a bottle of booze, a woman, and daily blunders. We want to live a little bit of him, nobody wants to be Bukowski – we just enjoy hearing the catastrophe.

Factotum was the first novel I read by Charles Bukowski,

When reading *Factotum* – you might think is this for real, this is what all the fuss is about? Yes, it is because you'll remember the story and maybe read it again.

I can equate many of Bukowski's days to my own and I imagine we all feel like him sometimes. At first you may want to reject his novels but soon you know you are onto something unique, no matter how trivial they seem, he does what he does, entertain.

These authors, these books, have simplicity. Other than John Fowles (he wrote books that only a few could attempt) I wouldn't say writing is their strength – the strength is their life they tell.

I have read many better books than these authors have written – they haven't hooked me on reading, they've hooked me on writing.

8

AN ENVELOPE IS ON MY table from the Debt Trustee.

I open the envelope – I'm free – the creditors have accepted the proposal.

I have legally evened the bank.

I call my wife at home in Cambodia.

I tell her to release the hundred thousand dollars I have hidden away, build a house on property she owns, lease it out for income – buy barren property as an investment in case of an emergency.

'Okay, Honey. When will you come home?'

I will go to work for a couple of months. Make our spending money.

My decision twenty months ago to challenge the bank is now done. I have a hundred thousand dollars to spend.

Every cent the bank lent I never spent, except to pay the interest and make investments, the remainder I stored in case I'd have to pay back the loan if the extortion failed.

Let me tell it this way – I'm against the system.

The dead machine inside us – is pop up – microscopic beginnings increasing in size, runs on a timer.

There are many dead machines inside us, sometimes we shut them down, sometimes they shut us down. Believe it, you already know there is a world inside us. You'd rather believe the God from above instead of the gods within.

I'm talking to you.

I could never have achieved this without being humble and patient. One year's work, plus what I'll make with the investments. Lazy you could say.

I won't see the money if all goes to plan. The money will be in dirt and rock – I may die but the dirt and rock will be here for my children. I've never intended to lavish myself in winnings, prop myself up. I just needed selfish time and security for my family – I'm tired of the system. I don't have to explain it, and I shouldn't have to explain what I do with my money – the corporation already knows and thus the problem.

I'd already taken thirty thousand in credit when I made the decision to be all in – it was then at my bedroom door that I felt the forlorn trip I'd be in.

All the tragedy, all the missteps, I blame on my decision to challenge the bank. I realize they are not connected, bad luck and good luck. I trust they are not connected but in the middle of a storm you believe you've done something wrong to bring on such thunder wind spark.

It is true since I made the decision to take the money my life has become frightening.

Will have calm now, I'll be able to sail across the sea find beautiful fruit, offer unique guidance, live free of the burden of wealth, and not lust the freedom of broke.

It sounds easy – sounds funny, the plan to escape.

A low interest rate on a credit line – pay the interest with credit, keep the rest in storage, claim near bankruptcy, make a proposal and get an interest free loan. And one last step; have little income, don't own anything – lucky for me, my wife owns much.

Easy money is when you don't realize how it happened, it just happened.

A plan is never easy, a jab to the head, a shot to the liver, a punch in the gut, a tired hand.

A businessman right or wrong can always say it was business – and then he can walk away.

Same with religion.

Same with sport.

Science.

Help me with the excuses – well, I have an excuse too; it was and is for word.

Thank you to the Bank for sponsoring me – I couldn't have done it without you. Spy, master, slave owner.

It was only business.

Monster of blood sucking, invest in them and you'll make money.

—

I confirm I will be at work in the oil fields in a week.

I inform Neha and Veronica I will be leaving as they've been expecting.

I have a direct line to the spirits, I needn't a middleman, I haven't labels.

Always tell a lie and always tell the truth.

I enjoy solitude in my room until Neha knocks.

'Come upstairs,' she tells me.

I do as I'm told – Neha and Veronica are in the kitchen, leaning against the counter, talking.

Veronica hugs me, pushing her tiny breasts against me, kisses me on the lips, invites me to stay for dinner.

Veronica mean – the first interest she's shown is a show for Neha.

As Neha leaves I can see sadness in her eyes. I sit and wait as dinner is delivered. Veronica enjoys a glass of wine while preparing the kitchen table.

We are having fun again and continue to visit after our meal.

She remarks she should quit smoking.

'Smoking is good for you!' I claim.

'No, where did you hear that?'

'I didn't hear it. I'm telling you smoking is good for you because you like it.'

'What else is good for me?'

'I don't know. I don't know what the majority of your body likes. You see it doesn't matter what your mind likes, it is what your brain likes, unless you are feeding your mind.'

'Are you feeding my mind?' She looks up from her phone while puffing her cigarette.

'If you're mind likes stories, I'm feeding it.'

'What do you feed your mind?' Veronica curious.

'My mind feeds me, and my body tries to reject it.'

'Feed your body some wine and forget about your mind.' She lifts the bottle and almost fills my glass.

We finish our dinner.

Her phone squeals. She goes to her room and talks.

Please stop pestering me . . . just rub against me, set your nipple to my chest. It has begun. I becoming the monster – the human – I've pulled you in before and now it is time to do it again...dummy.

I jot down my technique to quit smoking on a piece of paper.

If you want to quit smoking

I can help you. Cold Turkey.

Water is the answer – substitute water for nicotine.

Every time you are to light a cigarette – hit water, take to a bathtub, the shower, the swimming pool, the creek, or lake.

Take to water for three days.

By day four you're cured.

Stay away from old habits for a few weeks before returning to your regular life.

I'm about to place the paper with instructions to quit smoking under her cigarette package, then I rip the paper up as I remember she only smokes two to three cigarettes a day – unless she is going out to a party. This technique won't work for her; she smokes for fun, she has control.

I rinse dishes, let them soak in the sink.

I say good night, my glass of wine half finished.

I have challenged my wife and she has won. I have challenged my friend for rekindle and she has not stepped forward, she is a good friend.

I'm the loneliest man in an invisible world – when you aren't heard you wonder if you exist.

Invisible isn't like the book or the movie; it is attainable = like levitation, we exaggerate.

You can be seen unnoticed, or noticed unseen.

You can hide and use it to your advantage or you can walk in front of many eyes and none of them are the wiser. How do you make yourself invisible? Skill – you do what you can, if you want to be seen you'll be seen. Force the minds of others – let them make the decision you prefer.

—

I echo my evening to clear Neha's possible aching head. I was in bed early last night reading a book. I didn't even finish my glass of wine.

Neha knows her feelings are not spare.

She appears to speak truthfully too. 'Veronica is punishing me and you.'

How does she know about us?

'It is her job. She wants to know what is going on. She's good at it – she does it for fun.'

'Maybe she has a camera in here, perhaps a recording device.'

'She doesn't need all that. She can do better than that.'

'What is better than that?'

'Human.'

'What is human?'

'Me – and you.'

'You tell her everything?'

'No, but she knows. She can tell when we talk – saying nothing is as good as speaking. I used to ask about you before she began to notice and now I don't talk about you but she does, she knows, she questions me about what we do. I say nothing but she insinuates. She can see the way you talk to me so slow – you talk to me like no one else, your voice is so smooth.'

She can read us.

'She gave me your recipe – what does she expect?'

Her recipe is no good, too sweet and sour at the same time.

'Ha, ha.'

We embrace.

Relief. Neha smart, I considerate, I a fool = she congratulates me, we lay together not touching, enchanted, reflective – we knowing we have ended, there is nowhere else to go but inside each other.

I can't imagine more, today she has excelled my desire, and yet we haven't eclipsed our marriage vows.

It is two days away before I leave.

Neha, friendly; she doesn't have to clean my room she has no need, but she says she wants to.

I watch TV.

She packs up the vacuum cleaner, places it outside the door. She addresses me, 'You want this, you want this now?' meaning her body.

I don't speak. I don't move.

'I didn't think so,' she laughs.

'Come here,' I say.

'Let me go shower first. I will be back before I leave for home.'

Neha sometimes showers in Veronica's extra bath.

Relationships, I think we are good for each other, we are even, we always knew we were even.

Neha returns. Careful, maybe Veronica will be home soon.

Some kind of lesson – I pull Neha fast down on my lap.

'If you tried now I wouldn't stop you... I wouldn't enjoy it though, and I think you know that, so you won't. I can relax. Before, in the first days, I would have surrendered. I wouldn't have stopped you, like I said before. After days when I knew you, I wanted to enjoy everyday with you instead of twenty minutes romantically because then I'd never be able to enjoy you again. Now I have enjoyed you without guilt, without pressure, without nothing except exactly how I feel, and I feel good with you. I know it won't cross over, you aren't going to show up at my door, you aren't going to haunt me, nor will we have a fight. You will leave soon and when you come back I doubt you'll call and if you do I can say no or I can say yes. You will have time to decide if I'm worth it. Nothing will happen. Nor will I be hurt. An affair was over the first week, I was strong enough to tear you off, but that first day, that first night I was I....' She laughs. 'I can't say.'

'Me too, I didn't sleep that night. It was like I was together with you in mind, in energy.'

'You are right, it was me, as good as physical, wasn't it?'

'I don't know about that'.

'It was. It was all day, all night intense. You think you can make love to me all day and all night intense?'

'Yes, I could.'

'You can't because you can only have me for a half hour at most and then I'd be at home. So consider it now – it was as good as physical, wasn't it?'

'Maybe I can believe'.

'Maybe? You experienced and you loved it, and still you have moments – you see you are a great man, not weak – you think weak because you didn't ~~fuck~~ me for five-ten minutes, instead of what we have had for six weeks. Tell me now... which is better?'

'Fifteen minutes.' I laugh.

—

As great as the Great Gatsby was – the idea was better than the story.

Death money work.

Yet I complain about art? Art is the outlet of life, the inside of life – with no debt and a likable job, where would art come? Death was to come – death is to come – more common than oxygen, more abundant than water. Tragedy is the great life story.

Just live!

Give an example of how to live.

Talk it, draw it, write it, sing it, is nothing unless you can live it – set the example of how life can be lived – some kind of model results.

'Cliché,' Machine says.

Cliché, because good.

If I am one living in comfort, the rest of universe can follow an example.

To not ~~fuck~~ her and leave. To ~~fuck~~ her and leave, to ~~fuck~~ and carry on, to remain friends and no ~~fucking~~ – all cliché.

An affair is Number One cliché – to do on purpose to be different is again cliché.

No happy without sad.

No rich without poor.

If you are rich, what do you care? You care because you must defend the rich.

Comfortable isn't risk. You want risk, fun, adrenaline, Yes?

Comfort (Poise) is best.

Comfort (Cool) in adventure, comfort in tragedy, comfort in lust, comfort in love, comfort in job, comfort in battle....

Comfort not comfortable, if comfortable, the mist of envy will come.

Comfort (Calm) in your surroundings – if comfortable your surroundings will slowly or quickly dwindle, you won't even know it vanished until it's gone.

In comfort you are aware you do not take desperate action – you calculate, you observe, and if your surroundings do vanish quickly or slowly you put it in context you adapt, you are pleasantly surprised. You still cry, you still have sad, you still have euphoria.

Comfort without being comfortable – comfortable is lazy. Comfort is confidante strong.

Serene: call it spiritual if you like, alien, inner strength, angel, wind, tree, sun, as you like, comfort from above, around, maybe it comes from your mind.

The protected one.

Cliché!

If I'm to live poorly I am to be poor.

It may take your whole life – do what you like – if you must do something you dislike to accomplish what you like... so be it.

Complain, I want to hear it – in art. Do not live the example of your complaints.

For one to admit no found comfort is to begin to have comfort and to speak with a wide view.

Wisdom is the non-results.

Luck, the result.

Lust has ceased – Lake Wapa no longer intrigues.

My children, my wife, the jungle, the ocean, my desk, my home begins with my job in the oil field. I'm already at work in my mind, my money-making zone.

—

When I first slept on our property in Cambodia it seemed fine, almost sensational in the pouring rain.

We'd built a small four-room shelter.

The property was haunting only because the property was remote, the entrance long, narrow, dark, hidden unseen – neighbors distant away. The road to our place was desolate mostly, seldom passers passed by.

A scream would go nowhere.

Rats, lizards, insects, ocean breeze, distant storms of the sea.

Everyone was scared to stay on the property alone night or day. Overgrown over vegetation on three sides and an orchard on the fourth side.

No electricity at this time.

Frightened of machetes, robbery, and guns.

But mostly frightened of the unknown.

Some people call them ghosts.

The place was quiet, quiet enough to startle oneself.

On the up-side, relatives, friends, visitors, loved the quiet remoteness of the property.

We were happy when we started to build a new house – power lines – yeah, electricity. A new house we could protect ourselves. Comfort.

We were to build our house in two phases. We could live in phase one, as phase two was to be built.

During phase one the builder working alone on the property took a break from work, sat, drank water. A young woman came along and for twenty minutes conversed with him, asking him where he came from, what his intent was. This would be nothing exceptional except she was a ghost.

The builder was frightened in conversation though he never got up to leave. She the ghost wasn't menacing but, he was afraid, paralyzed – he had only one option and that was to converse with her.

From then on, he didn't like to be alone on the property.

I don't know his game.

Phase one of our house built, we moved in.

The new house was worse than the shelter as there wasn't an excuse; the shelter you could blame many things for fright.

Being outside or in the shelter the fear of a ghost is just the fear of not being secure. Haunted of the fear you made and the noises you heard and what you couldn't see.

In the new house you didn't have this excuse.

As I was to sleep I was tapped on the shoulder. I looked around laid back down. Clear as day, she spoke, 'L Ce,' in a soothing calm, perfectly toned voice, 'Come here. L Ce, come here.' A voice so recognizable I thought it was the voice of my wife.

Honestly, I thought my wife was in another room but she wasn't. The voice called my name again. I went back into the bedroom, sure my wife was joking me. She wasn't joking – she was fast asleep.

Like a game of hide and seek the voice came again. 'L Ce.' Lost, frantic – crazy – I'm searching for an invisible being.

Confused. I settled down and slept.

I wasn't the only one. My wife claimed she also heard voices; she sometimes asked me why I called her when I never did.

Bring on the real chance of robbery and theft, the ghost goes up a notch.

If I drank alcohol at least I could sleep, not the best security. The spirit was slowly killing me, at least I could sleep badly if I drank. I didn't know which was better, sober but frightened all night and then sleep the day, or drink, sleep numb, and suffer all day. As I look back it would have been better to sleep the day and stay awake at night. It never works like that.

I can talk about another demon called drink – another story – they all play the same game – to win without rules. You could say it was the vast inner life inside my body that liked booze and produced the voices, the fear, and the ghost, except I wasn't the only one hearing a ghost.

It shows that unsuspecting events in your life drive you to other terrible measures.

Live with your own fright, no, I couldn't do it.

I needed a change.

Phase two construction of our house complete.

Damn if I was going to be terrified of a ghost in our finished home.

I made a plan. Yes, it came to me one day – the inner universe is transferred to the outer universe. Create an atmosphere that if you were a ghost you'd be awestruck.

This idea is just as implausible as a Ghost on the property – I know, but it couldn't hurt. Would it hurt to have a fun, lovable atmosphere in our home for our ghost to bask in?

I concluded it was myself. I needed to stop being crazy. Banish inner strife. I'm not a bad man but I could be a lot better.

Be honest. Be respectful. Take care of your ghost. Not be guilty of life's unseen, the invisible stuff you think nobody knows, except the spirit does know.

Live right is the easiest explanation.

You don't have to live with your wicked ways.

Be better, live better.

The ghost is ours. Give it no reason to growl. We now laugh at our ghost.

Prison comes in many forms. Accept it happily.

9

PATIENCE LACKING, I'M parked in Veronica's driveway early morning.

I'd like to thank Veronica for my stay.

Yesterday I missed her the entire day.

I stayed at my mother's last night.

Neha arrives early at Veronica's to begin work.

She greets me.

I ask her if she's heard from Veronica.

'She won't be coming home until later this afternoon. She's to drive up to the resort for business.'

'Where is she now?' I ask, bewildered.

Neha hesitates.

'She might be at your friend's place.'

'My friend's place?'

'Yes, your friend who she is buying a mountain bike from.'

She's been gone all night.

'Go see. Maybe she stayed with him, maybe she stayed at the office.'

Incredible – no, not incredible, monstrous – the two of them, slacks down.

I go to Tru's first.

What kind of pain have I been handed? There is no pain, there is no shock, there is numb. I'm not dizzy or hallucinogenic. I'm remote control. I haven't any kind of story. I accept I'm driving to a scene of brazen behavior.

I'm not so brash. I know I can briefly see Tru's alley driveway where the forest thins if I turn onto the service road along the highway.

Veronica's car is parked in the back driveway of his home.

It is more than a bicycle, my mind twirls.

I turn around on the service road and start driving back.

I slow for one more viewing.

Veronica is now outside, smoking. Tru makes his way past her with a broom to remove snow off her car. She butts her cigarette, then places the cigarette butt in her cigarette packet.

I slowly speed away.

Unbelievable is not what is seen – it is my timing to view this astounding exhibition that is incredible.

Maybe they are smarter than I am because I haven't torture, I haven't jealousy. I only have Lake Wapa. I must be the one to ask them – they cannot tell me. I will be the desperate one, the victim, if I ask, if I tell them I know. Yes, it will be secret until they – one of them – tells me. And how will I best react? I'd laugh. No, that would be mean. I'd have to be considerate.

Veronica has let the bad come in – she negated her God – she, animal, tasted instinct, she failed or triumphed. Don't ask me or her mouth, ask what she dreams when alone.

Sure... the ugly, the mean, is what I sometimes dream, it doesn't matter whatever that attraction shred tells you.

We did love for hours, battle for days, ignore for months. Could I marry her? Sure, I could marry many – children though? Ha ha, no.

Children. This is the true barometer.

I'm not that smart. I haven't a skill in this ancient world. We the human are just beyond building a fire.

Tru said 'I don't intimidate him.' I don't understand. That makes us friends?

Tru is one of the few that speaks as he thinks. They take it or they walk away. Some challenge him. I've watched him beat much bigger men. I watched him fight much smaller men.

He doesn't have rules. His rule is if he has fear, he acts.

I will speak with him again.

Let her have this break of grace with Tru as I have had with Neha.

Tru. The Brute.

Veronica ...what about Veronica? Less human all of a sudden because she is with my friend?

And now I don't scream, I don't run, I laugh, I love because all my insensitivities before are gone. It was a fear that was built, not pre-installed. The reality, the actuality of it, doesn't hurt, doesn't matter – it is a not ill gotten, it is not life altering. It has no emotional effect other than stunned, and even now I think not stunned. It was a set up; buy a bicycle. I letting them meet, it is a gift, a gift of my Ruins. My feelings have long evaporated of interest – this was my entertainment, an adventure in humdrum.

I have claimed the past insignificant. Even the past here in Lake Wapa was not my life, it was send off to life, my platform to bounce to the world. Lake Wapa visit and smile because Lake Wapa can't hurt me, only a picture to laugh, reflect, smile.

You are wrong, Machine.

She isn't the muse, she is only notes, possibly a short story – a learning.

Well go ahead and learn.

You've spent the time, now do the work – write.

It doesn't matter, her name – go to a place and meet a woman and a story will come.

I return to Neha to confirm.

Neha answers, 'I saw them kiss, here in the kitchen. Are we any better than them?'

Same, everyone is the same, except some people make larger mistakes. The only people who are different are the ones that have lost reality, the sick… they are not the same.

Neah resumes, 'Veronica doesn't even like him – she loves the adventure is all.'

I still have nothing to add.

Neha continues, 'Veronica has always been my friend.'

Neha pauses – and answers her own question.

'Is it my business to tell you – you have already moved on, you will be gone from Lake Wapa today and I will still be here with Veronica. I've given you this gift and I think you will leave without making noise. A year from now I won't care. Months from now I won't care.'

One more time.

My hands grasp her, she turns away, lays on her stomach on the couch – I can finish her here now. I step away, shut the door.

Am I advanced human or half-animal? I am the unseen. We have already made love, we just need to take the physical steps – so it doesn't matter.

I'm learning death.

I can write about women my whole life, adventure everyday. Sometimes I can fulfill my desire.

Remember we are traveling backwards, not forwards – we are just living the results.

I can complain about the banking system, the corporate blanket everyday but to write about it seems mundane – fit in, or drop out. I prefer drop out – no bank account, no corporate protection.

It is the same sensation as when I left Veronica naked – if you work long enough and hard enough you have it, you are done. Move on, start again.

This night. My mind discovers Nano signals, an acceleration of Dynamic Affect.

Signals marked black, white, grey, popping up in patterns is my best reenactment.

My Machine firing up, I think I can see inside my brain.

Nanotechnology.

Is levitation coming soon? Matter leaving and entering my body again.

Nano-bots have infiltrated. They used to fade in the shade and relax, tame, the timer has unleashed them for the unintelligent information I'm receiving. Machine says they're intelligent, sure they're intelligent for the service they've been programed – however, they are making my life difficult, assigning erratic decisions.

Write, live right, and richness will come.

The Nanos know.

What is a great man if the Nano's are helping him? I ask Machine.

If you want to be great, you have already failed.

I have been programmed for failure at many things and other things success... destiny. I haven't control, no matter how hard I try to fail I succeed and the opposite. I can practice and try but will ultimately fail – some things we can't do wrong and others wrong, wrong, wrong, after three you might want to try something else.

They are running in your blood, intelligent machines.

I'm falling down. Stand up, let the outside nature infiltrate the human inside world.

Nanos on timers – you were a kind of ape, in the future tell me what you'll be. In the long past you were energy, some kind of angel. In the near future will you be an angel again?

Made by machine, you float, held by gravity in the body of an advanced ape.

Leave the body, levitation, astral projection, let the Nano lone.

Spend more time in your mind

Nano flows through your blood, circles the meat of your brain.

I don't know what the machine is but in our current time in history nano-science can relate.

If you understand shaman and magical drink you can visit predawn.

—

Amazon Peru (Before I met my wife)

I asked to see Shaman.

Challenge him.

Surrender him.

I drink.

Shaman drinks the drink to cause vomit, to hallucinate.

Nothing, rest, wings flap around my head, dinosaur bird circles tilts back my head, swooning in.

I close my eyes so not to hallucinate.

Shaman vomits.

I crawl into the Shaman's head as he chants and fans, he's empty inside, a skeleton, I see out of his eyes.

I lay to rest and move warp speed from my mind past my brain ... the sound of zoom.

Purple night, florescent blue, colors far more advanced than I've seen.

I don't see with my eyes or with my mind but as the universe. I travel as an asteroid when life first traveled to Earth and now I travel back to where life first came. I wait for another zoom . . . and before I give up I'm transported again through live colors amongst stars to Earth.

The Shaman sleeps now and I muddle around the jungle for an hour before resting in the hammock, super powered with the girl I've trekked in the jungle with.

I know that Jesus isn't matter in my brain; I may say I look to Buddha but it is my ability to place people in place for a reason that is unique. Many people placed are the same people with another face. Jesus is nowhere to be found, I'm free to explore my natural life and leave the killers behind.

Woke up, two days to recuperate from when I drank with Shaman.

I have more power in the pen. Words on paper fly to minds. I'm finding glitches in the universe and destroying false remedies.

The thrill tonight... is what I've waited, wanted.

How can I thank this girl? I want to see ~~fuck~~ her again even if it may kill me, I'm seriously close to death as it is and I think this may be what death is... extreme ecstasy in misery, fumbling for energy even though all energy is taken, absorbing the rush of life while on the verge of death.

Yes, I'm protected from disease... it isn't enough.

Clouds falling, I must use a condom or not, dangerous, never content until I find a woman where a condom is never a question or consequence. Pleasure isn't had with a gift, I can't have fun without taking responsibility – if I press a button the button comes with a price and every foot print I leave is a dent in something else. When I think, the sensation inhabits another with thoughts and reaction.

Words have the most power, but it is thoughts that process words.

The woman crunches a plastic condom wrapper before flinging it behind the bedroom dresser. I'm smiling, laughing inside, thinking she's kidding and I'll have my way. I provide another condom. She accepts the condom into a hard fist and fires the prophylactic against the wall. I look behind the television. I can't find the protection I need. Not so funny now. She isn't kidding.

She thinks that if I use a condom I'm not with her 100 percent. True, I am not.

It is that package on the floor that keeps life or death.

Simplicity.

I'm wrong, she is right – no child.

I visit Shaman again, when I travel inside his head I stop.

His head is full of insects, worms, and maggots. I can't view with his eyes.

I focus on a tree across the river for an hour, telling myself all is a hoax.

In the morning I look to the tree across the river but the tree isn't across the river; the tree is in front of me. My jungle time done, I've crossed the river. My trip has concluded. Peru is finished. I can achieve everything I've sought.

What I sought is freedom to write, wealth to travel... and a lover to fly through the universe with.

You can ask me, which is the most difficult?

Writing is the easiest; in prison I can write, if poor I can write, if rich I can write, if incapacitated I can write – drug addicted, failed, miserable, healthy, acclaimed, successful, completely at peace I can write.

I have one friend, one lover, one luxury, and one liberty, the ability to live in my mind and write.

Wealth can harm and assist, a lover the same.

—

Spirited Drink

Never thought I'd complete a short story on alcohol, maybe I haven't, too difficult. Read:

'Beautiful is a free mind – dance?' she said to me.

I wanted to speak, 'Yes, dance,' as I accepted the flower bouquet I'd paid her for.

She disappeared from the street to the alley and ran into the field, but not before an entrusting gleeful smirk, most consuming of my sudden desire.

Sleep, eat, work – entertain is to walk to the field were the beautiful woman ran.

Out in my yard to breath the air of the evening wind, an arrow softly punctures the side of my neck. I look around, I cannot find who released this bow-arrow.

In minutes I feel pain.

It is a poisoned tipped arrow.

The only cure I think is Spirited Drink – maybe two drinks, as that's the limit, as long as I'm not inebriated.

Cured, the poison has been released. I feel relaxed, consumed in thought with explanations of problems thrown away.

Next night I walk the street to the alley towards the field. I cannot find the beautiful woman that sold me the flowers.

The following evening as I return from work, an arrow strikes my shoulder blade – I retreat to my property but not before another arrow strikes my leg.

I need to relax, take the poison out.

Four drinks for two arrows.

The next day, three more arrows, two hit and the third arrow I jump in front of, – struck by the third – I have six drinks this day for three arrows.

On my day off, I proceed to find the culprit with the bow and find the beautiful woman I'd bought the bouquet of flowers from.

She rests in a tree with a bow and arrows.

I want to rip the bow from her hands – I don't. I want to scold her – I don't.

I surrender, she slings back the bow string, her lips smooch, the arrow sails and strikes above my heart – the pain feels wonderful coming from her. Two more arrows are strung as I stand in front of her.

'Go home,' she says, 'Before I poison you more.'

'Why?' I ask.

'Because I like you. Go now before you are unable to have the strength to find me again.'

I cure myself half the night with Spirited Drink.

Stumble at work.

I've been finding her earlier in the day with as many as ten arrows aimed. I avoid some, most strike.

One thing I know, I must take out the poison.

I enjoy the poison more than the drink – the drink has become a casualty of the poison.

Before I'm to find her this day I notice everything grey and dying around my land.

Colors and bright smells have fled.

Shaken, I admit maybe I can't see her anymore.

As night comes I find and follow her, she leads me close to the mountain and asks, 'You having fun?'

'Extremely confusing fun,' I answer.

'Is it pleasure, or horror, this fun you speak of?'

'Horrifying pleasure,' I answer.

She says, 'Don't resist if you like it so much.' The first arrow misses my leg, she looks at her bow, she tries again. The next three arrows connect before a fourth arrow misses. She snaps an arrow in half curses.

She slings a new arrow. It strikes my waist. The last arrow, with much time and aim, strikes my forehead. She runs to the mountainside.

Grouchy, shaking, trouble to eat, today I'm too tired to even visit the beautiful woman with a cure for my ailing, but I must to endure the rest of the day.

Late afternoon I search for the girl with the bow.

She is no longer in the alley, the street, the tree, nor the field.

I go near the mountain.

A Beast is near the mountain.

The Beast has inhabited her. Holding her bow, arrows, and wearing her clothing. I ask the Beast what happened to the beautiful woman who shot the softest arrows. The Beast answers, 'There was never a beautiful woman, only a vision in your mind created by you for something you think you like. It was always me, the ugly Beast, and soon if I keep striking you with the poison arrow you too will grow haggard, grouchy, look and sound as me.'

I look at my face in the pond and true I'm becoming not so fair, not so nimble, not so happy.

'But if I don't take out the poison I cannot sleep, I cannot move, I cannot think, I cannot work well, I become irritated. The poison of the arrow makes me sick, but heals as well.'

The Beast answers, 'The arrow is the cure, the drink is poison. Accept the arrow and the pain for a few days and slowly you'll see.'

The Beast strikes me with an arrow before chasing me up the mountain where there is no drink to cure.

The next day as I walk down the mountain, The Beast strikes me with two arrows and chases me back up the mountain.

I walk, ponder, accepting the pain of the arrows.

After three days, The Beast allows me to walk free to my home, but not before striking me yet again with an arrow.

I accept the pain, go to work, take care of choirs, and after a few days I try new things, plant a garden – visit an old friend.

After a month I go to visit the Beast and thank him.

The Beast isn't to be found.

I return home, my leg is struck with an arrow. The arrow has come from my garden.

The beautiful woman laughing with the bow – I want to run, shout, 'Who are you?' to the Woman, or Beast?

She speaks, 'Go to the mountain accept this pain, and come back home tomorrow. I'll wait here for you.'

I accept the pain, wander the mountain, read the sky, speak with trees waving in the wind, eat the green leaves of nature and taste the fresh smell of rain. All has happened this night, thunderstorm and sunshine in the morning.

The beautiful woman tends to my garden. I greet her, she hands me a bow arrow and speaks. 'Your turn, we each have a bow and arrow.'

We are equal.

We become adept at missing the arrow and when we are hit by the poison arrow we laugh, accepting the pain, and begin all over again.

She speaks, 'I was inhabited by a Beast when I drank Spirited Drinks to release the poison of the guilt of striking you, my beauty gone, my spirit gone. I fled to the lake to heal as I could no longer shoot my arrows straight, though you assisted in jumping in front of them.'

'Where is the Beast now?' I ask.

'Hibernating. The Beast may or may not come again, depending if we need to be taught. The Beast will hibernate if we've learnt. The Beast sleeps, but if woken the Beast can stay awake for many days, months, or even decades.'

10

THE COMPANY I WORK for book me in a hotel room. They rent a black suburban SUV (I've always disliked large black SUV's – when I see them I want to shoot them with a gun; they represent a get out-of-the way attitude I detest) I will drive up to the worksite eight hours north. I'm to spend two days in the city of Calgary, filling out forms, complete a hearing test, a drug and alcohol test, and pre-job meeting before I travel north.

Something is eating me.

A con, to do a job for seven years, this is my eighth. I was to work for five years and move on. Five of anything becomes stale. My limitations have begun. My limitations have always been visible to a strong eye and invisible to the majority. I can still pass on reputation; I will have to do something with my wit so I'm congratulated, remembered.

The strength to do a job I'm not intended to do is beyond any professional, schooled or trained – it is empowering and it is also destabilizing – the power to accomplish anything and the disillusion of doing nothing.

Wrecked!

The novel and poet is the release of stored energy, an adult's version of a child's imaginary games.

If I do not work at this job what will I do for money?

Suffer!

Veronica knows this about me – Tru knows this about me – even Neha knows this about me.

I will suffer to play my addiction to imagination.

I have no dream job.

'Grow up!' Machine says.

Why grow up? No adult is smarter than a kid – they just live.

My author friend knows best – take something in return for your work.

Went out late night to buy some supplies and dinner.

The Machine plays video games. The ghost reappears, or perhaps an alien dropped a car in front me as clear as the sky, a green light through the intersection – certainly the intersection was clear before the possessed car appeared, aimed at the front end of the SUV. I swerved. The car slammed the rear panel of the SUV – a good jolt.

A ghost, an alien, set on destruction, as I could see no driver of the car. Even after the accident I never had a glimpse of the driver. The police arrived instantly as they were near the intersection.

I parked the SUV at a petrol station and proceeded to walk across the intersection to the car that smashed into me but the police officer directed me to stay with my vehicle.

Ten minutes later the car was loaded onto a flatbed truck.

I filled out my witness statement; the police officer said it wasn't my fault; a woman drove her car into mine.

A haunting has started before the project.

I should never have driven a vehicle I despise. My hate has turned back on me – don't hate. Let them (drivers of large black SUV) drive what they like. Move out of the way and let them be.

The ghost come, the video game, the spell, or is it? I, pure luck, I saved myself with a swerve of the wheel from injury.

The SUV damaged. The Company rents a van for me to drive.

I've gone back to work – finance, death, romance. Work is supposed to please (making money is supposed to do that).

To stop when traveling a downhill slope takes much power – to go back up-hill is a struggle.

The best is midstream, you forget this comfort when you're busy, ego driven, ascending, or cursing as you descend. The climb up is the adventure, it is when you stop and picnic that is serene. Maybe you're starting your climb and you stop and rest, this is peace, or when you're half-way and build a shelter – stay awhile, this is nice – or near to the top, such glory, such charm as you know you're almost there. When you reach the top, a minute of reflection – down the hill, go slow, enjoy it like you did on the adventure up.

Complain, complain, nobody hears you! Stop complaining.

On top of the mountain you hear no echo, at the bottom of the mountain you hear no echo. Only somewhere in-between can an echo be heard.

Back home to my wife and kids after this – the story I write is nothing – money is what they want. I need change. You yourself can only understand – your voice will not be heard by others depending on you. If you are not happy those around you will not be happy as well.

Never depend on others. Don't wait. Go make a life. God. Your nation. No, you can't get caught up in that trap.

We seek others – we cry when we are young, we cry when we are old, we need others, don't rely on them.

You can't do it yourself, it's true – you'll die. But hey, live or die.

Cry, dance, laugh.

—

I attend the pre-job and orientation with a familiar face, a Polish guy named Arnold. He worked his first project as a Safety Advisor two years ago with me. Arnold is recently divorced – once he separated from his wife he quit his job as Derrick-man on the drilling rig and began pursuing a safety career. At fifty-six years old he's looking for safety to take him to retirement.

Arnold is a handsome guy – about fifteen pounds overweight – a smiling charmer with eyes that twinkle. Women enjoy him or keep their distance. Guys are the same; they put up with him or laugh with him. The best thing about Arnold if you are with him he'll do anything for you but if you are against him he can make it much worse for you. We laugh and argue like good friends do. Arnold will be what I won't, a Safety Advisor – he strives to be the best, he takes courses on his days off.

When not taking courses, Arnold lets loose on substances and dating making up for his married days – good on him, but watch out!

I can feel the fire burning.

I take no courses... don't care to become one of the guys. I keep a professional distance, don't attempt to better my safety credentials. I can look up everything in a book or call another safety mind.

We follow each other north to location. Core drilling rigs, lease roads, construction, and contractors servicing the rigs. All happenings in our respective areas will be reported and responded, investigating incidents, checking compliance and procedures have been followed.

A nice job – when all goes well.

Northern Alberta – Muskeg, cold, work camps. Dreams won, dreams fade. They call it 'Paradise' a trip north and you'll be finically saved. If you stay too long in the north you'll die in the trap.

No politics, like most I'm here to make money and move on to my own desires and beliefs.

We are replacing two Safety Advisors who were run off for differences of opinion. It is the end of winter season for this project as spring is coming – The Energy Company will only keep a few drilling rigs on location as the ground thaws and the roads on the muskeg become impassable. It is now early February. I will be lucky to make it to mid-March.

Camp holds thirteen hundred staff and guests. I have my own room, washroom, television, Wi-Fi, and a desk. Breakfast, lunch, dinner, served down the hall in the dining area – as many deserts as you like. Exercise room, confectionary, and recreation room. Camp is loaded with security, the halls monitored by camera and patrolled by security guards. A gated community you must check in for entry and exist. No alcohol is allowed. Sex is allowed I suppose as condoms are sold, you often-hear stories of one or two women setting up shop. I heard a story from housekeeping that most of the sex they discover is guy on guy.

Stunned!

Some like camp as you don't need money and everything is done for you. I prefer a hotel, when I shut the hotel room door I'm gone, lost to the working world. You are never free at camp. This camp is nice. The food is good, I have no complaints. Any camp where you have your own toilet is a good camp.

The industry is like free money – I have no education, I have no conviction. All I have to do is make busy.

The price is high if you believe in the dream – you may wake up and find your life is missing.

Before we are to start our nightshifts, we must attend a course on drugs and alcohol in the work place. We will receive a certificate when we have finished the two-day course.

Arnold failed his drug test for this project last year, he'd tested positive for THC. His one-year ban from this site is now over. The positive test for marijuana didn't stop him from working on other projects with different oil companies.

We attend the workshop on drugs in the workplace – the climax the kicker: 'If you are off work for the weekend...' They gave an example of how wasted you could be,

They told us: "We can drink alcohol Friday night, all day Saturday and all day Sunday, and on Monday morning we'll be fine to work. But if you smoke marijuana all weekend you won't be able to perform your job?"

This is the way the oil company runs their business – the truth is the exact opposite – the only truth is you'll pass the alcohol test and fail the drug test. But I can assure you going on a drinking bender will not result in a safe, productive, healthy environment.

I laugh. I don't protest. I accept the bull for the paycheck.

I receive the diploma for my ability to recognize drugs in the workplace.

Stuff it all crumpled up in the sleeve of my suitcase.

Soon marijuana will be legal in Canada. I don't know what will happen then, maybe the opposite: smoking pot is good, drinking is bad?

By the time I'm finished the two day course I will have been paid two full days plus my travel day, pre-job, and orientation day, four days' pay and I haven't even set foot on a rig. Despite the motor vehicle accident I'm taking the positive road.

My author friend is day shift. I will see him at our crossover meetings – day shift and night shift meet daily before and after our shifts.

My positivity is in need. Maybe I can survive one last safety job before I move on to a different endeavor.

Work is like putting up a window that offers the view the payee wants to see.

Work is lies to keep your job.

I've seen the honest person keep their mouth shut to keep their job. I've seen the dishonest open their mouth to keep their job.

We can find faults in anyone.

Stay off the radar – if you are on the radar fault will be found. If they come after you, you better have built something – favors and tales, otherwise you will have no lifejacket. Build support, quiet favors. Gossip is killer. A solid reputation is key.

Find a job and make it easy. My goal is to work extremely hard when I need to, be responsible, create an environment to strive in, thus freeing up time to write or at least jot down poems, one liners, make quotes.

My attitude is like the Energy Company, false smiles, lies, and optimistic confessions all to keep my paycheck in good standing.

The Company Man, Rig Manger, Rig Crew, Rig Servicing, and the Safety Department, you must dance their steps. You have to know the person you are making the decisions with, somethings are kept in-house and others need to be reported. Reporting can lose your job, not reporting can lose your job. If you report you better have support and if you don't report you better have support. If you cross someone you are dead, they will wait for you to make a mistake and take their turn, to turn you in.

If you aren't busy, pretend you are busy.

If you are liked they like you coming around.

If you aren't liked you won't know what the hell is going on, you'll create and search for answers, you'll be looked on as the enemy.

If you show no harm the crew will give you answers, they will do the safety for you, all you have to do is record.

Arnold and I perfect – even when we fuck up!

We cover for each other knowing the other's territory. We work hard, we start early every day, and if we can finish early, we do – if we have to stay late, we do. Nobody says shit to us because we work hard. Most chase freedom. Arnold and I create freedom.

When you have a project like this with good people you can be sure you'll have pain on another project soon. I was dammed two projects in failure in a row before this one – all my crispness gone.

Let's be truthful, you create the end yourself. I wasn't interested and that infiltrated my work. I let others direct my action.

Now I'm prepared for any direction, ready, willing – direct control, not chasing, this works in all aspects of life.

Produce a good environment and if all fails... it was to be no excuse.

All these things that I have spoken matter, but what really matters and what I truly care about is nobody gets hurt – protect the workers and the public.

Safety Advisor is not a liked position. When you work as a Safety you think you are liked, they tell you they like you. It never occurs to you that you must be the only one liked.

You are put in a pot of dislike until you prove yourself and then you as an individual are a good person – one in ten. At first though they think about you wrong. If you screw up it is just another Safety Advisor, if you do well you are an individual, Safety Advisor has nothing to do with it. The Safety Advisor bright light never shines positive, you as the individual can.

11

WHEN I RECEIVED THE call, I didn't fall down – I knelt to one knee in grief. It was different when I received the call about my Nephew. I was numb, there was no rush of adrenalin, nor release, or frustration – I was still when I heard the news of my Nephew. It was said he was missing and they were searching, still I knew he was gone, except it is different because underneath it all is belief, but I would not say the Boy is missing, I'd say he is gone and my emotions gone too.

Now as I hear this it is a huge shock of adrenalin.

Tru is dead.

Of all the people it is Neha who called me.

'How?' I asked

'Badly.'

'How bad?'

'Beat, Burnt, OD'd – simultaneously.'

'And you? How are you?' I ask.

'Me, I'm alive.'

'Who did it?'

'Veronica is gone too.'

'Gone? What do you mean gone?'

'Her business, her homes, all gone, sold.'

'Where did she go?'

'She never said, never told anyone. She asked me to bring my things to the office in town on Friday and on Monday a new owner walked in. I started working for them. The new owner bought the company a week ago. They'd made offers to buy before but she always said no, now she said yes. She took her car and drove away I suppose. She disappeared. Sold everything in secret and left, days before he was murdered. I drove over to her house on Monday because her phone was disconnected. Her house was all locked up... neighbors said a moving truck was there the day before.'

'Wild. Her family doesn't know?'

'What family? She has no relatives left in Lake Wapa. I know her as well as anyone in this town. Vanished.'

'Is she dead too?'

'The police say she's alive, but that is all they will say.'

—

At work I find is a place of peace – in my room at night not so much – work can have its benefits. I resume my working ways.

Work is relationships.

You want me to talk about work – it is boring.

Safety

The oil company give gifts for the person who writes the best safety cards (a pocket size card that the worker fills out about hazard or a safety correction). A driller wins the award twice – the reason he writes the most and best safety cards is because he's so high on 'Meth' during his shift that he not only drills the fastest, he writes the fastest, and thinks of subjects to write the fastest. His mind very creative, I like him, but at times I think his eyes are about to pop out of their sockets. The onsite Company Man and the Rig Manger love him and his are crew afraid, afraid of losing their jobs if they cross him.

Thanks to the reckless driller I also receive an award (a jacket) because the most safety cards were handed in from the rig I look after. It goes like that, the Safety department rewarded, the Company Man proud, the Rig Manger congratulated, and the Boardroom clapping.

—

I've met an Interesting Woman at work.

After I heard the news about Tru and Veronica. I explained to Interesting Woman what I'd heard.

Interesting Woman looked at me and said, 'You are that used to death, that you can say it so calm like that?'

'I'm not used to death – I'm used to hearing it . . . that is all,' is what I replied to Interesting Woman.

Interesting Woman is funny – outrages smiles, stop and stare sentences. She is pale dark, African, Arabic, European, she can be many things in many lights one could say she is South American. She is Canadian.

She works emergency rescue in the plant. Even though the plant is in Arnold's area I visit often – a couple of small core rigs are in the plant. I visit for tea or lunch in a small cafeteria I have access to. Sometimes I visit with her at camp and other times I invite her to sit in my truck. We attend meetings together – whenever an excuse to meet for coffee or pie, we met.

She is quiet, she isn't shy. When she speaks, it is important.

At first, I engaged her smile, her body language, now I check her breast and ass... mysterious she has me.

I visit with my author friend on the phone or in person daily. He's my cross shift.

'Sometimes I want to have sex with the worst women,' my author friend confides.

I know the truth – I've been thinking of Interesting Woman, I'd never admit this to my author friend. He'll have to figure it out with his own eyes.

He tells me I never have to work again, just invest and write. He wants to travel, ~~fuck~~ with two Russian women, and I want one really good African woman.

He laughs. 'When will this happen. When can we do this?'

I haven't an answer, money first, travel and woman second.

My author friend is halfway to investment freedom, investment security where he has enough invested that the littlest movement up on his investment nearly meets his daily needs.

I ask him, why me? Why do you tell me these things?

'Because you have done it, and soon you'll be able to do it again. Write, travel, invest,' he says.

'And what about ~~fuck~~? You didn't say ~~fuck~~ – you said write, travel, invest. But you didn't say ~~fuck~~ at the end of the list?'

'I don't know, maybe we love our wives' too much.'

Maybe we have always been wrong. Sometimes a poet doesn't know how to live. A true poet would go the opposite, love first, travel second, poetry third, and never invest.

My author friend loves his wife but when he is at camp too long he forgets.

He'll say, 'I hate being married, it is suffocating.' Co-workers look at him insanely when he says such things out loud because they perceive goodness and truth from him. At the same time this truth annoys others – they dislike perfect. He is not perfect but he knows right from wrong. If the co-workers knew the conversations we have they'd be shocked – he is a writer, writers are like this, soft to the world but hard, very hard in the core.

Sometimes, I tell him, you have to go away and fuck some woman, get it out of your system, at a place and with a person that won't come back on you. A person that you'll forget when you need to say you never cheated. An afternoon, a morning, perhaps an evening of sex, then you move on – go ~~fuck~~ two, three women. Take a rest before you come home in case your wife wants to ~~fuck~~ with you too because maybe you haven't ~~fucked~~ her in weeks, but that time when you drain yourself with another women you can be sure it is the day your wife wants to fuck too.

'Sometimes I think the stories you write are fantasy,' my author friend comments.

My fantasies can't compete with my reality. If you want your marriage to work, go have fun. Here at work, I don't know if it is the place.

'Maybe we have to go away together,' the author suggests.

'Tell our wives we are going away, they will suspect it anyway. If we don't ~~fuck~~ around they'll wonder what is wrong with us. They will be happy and will prove us wrong that we went away because they'll prove the best honey is in their cave.'

'You are right. I think my wife wants me to go away and travel so I'm happy.'

Yes, they don't want to be bothered all the time, they hope we go ~~fuck~~ but they can't speak the words. Though my wife does speak the words, 'Go find a girlfriend'.

'Everyone says don't have sex at work but everyone does.'

'Not everyone.'

'True, I have never.'

'Neither have I.'

'It is good to talk like this.'

It is good to write about this.

He is a very honest man. He knows what it will take to be happy – he happy, his wife happy, his children content. And to him he will feel like he is living, has lived. He admits he doesn't know if he writes really well or terrible, all he knows is he enjoys writing and he is paid for it.

I near fell over when I asked Interesting Woman her dream – her dream is to write a book on spirituality, to live on another continent. I almost thought she was kidding or possible tricking me but no, she was speaking as she's always sought.

She says that I can't handle the truth.

What truth?

'Quiet, I can't tell you, someone is listening,' is how she responded.

I want to go find this truth. Sometimes when I think about her I leave my body and merge with hers. She told me of some kind of fire flying love – our unknown traveling parts join together in the universe. Connect – I feel this with her – I've heard of all kinds of bizarre things from women, however, this is the first time that I actually believe our bodies are connecting in the universe. You may say this is the same as with Neha – it is not the same.

Interesting Woman is telling me we have been connected and will continue to be over generations, in different forms, we've made love a million times, we are reoccurring. She is the woman that I see clear every few years in every continent like an old friend with many faces but always the same smile.

We have not been alone together. We have only made slight touches. We have not made plans. We have only conspired through open-ended sentences.

I know there is something between us and the physical journey to reach our spiritually would just be that and then we would separate, go on our way. If true or not true, if true we'd meet again and if not true we may meet again – the feeling, the ferocity will tell the truth if we are true as one.

Interesting Woman wants to go on a spiritual journey. Hike spiritual hills all over the world.

She asks me if I'm up for it, if I would like to take this journey with her.

Spiritual, travel, writing – perhaps romance, life altering – I want to expand on this spiritual adventure, make love in this spiritual journey, maybe this will take me to another stage.

My mind is wild. I can see us in the future meeting every year, every six months, for a spiritual journey.

This is the mind, this is the test.

Have I met the tease to destroy my life or the sun that brings me Utopia?

Is Utopia worth the chance?

Perhaps I'll never know – and if I find Utopia, why would I tell.

It travels like that. I've forgotten Neha.

I've left Veronica or maybe she has left me.

When I return to my wife I think I won't contact this spiritual dream, this Interesting Woman until I'm free traveling, or back to this wild country with fences for humans, fences for animals and soon fences for thoughts. Will I be disciplined for thinking about her?

The Astral Plane...

When she told me I can't handle the truth it was the most profound because I want to think I can – yet she is right, I will mold the truth to fit my scheme, much like earth we've developed to fit into the scheme of earth.

Hidden is our truth.

This Interesting Woman is the second kind of love. The first kind is warmth where you learn, you play – like Neha, like Veronica. The third kind is the dangerous kind, the organism you've never met, the one in a billion kind.

First love is friend's play – comfortable, sometimes embarrassing love. This is the love that we have all experienced. Sometimes they become our wives our ex-wives.

Second is love you understand, you are not embarrassed. All the parts fit perfect.

Third is the dangerous – jumping over the cliff, maybe live, maybe die. Complete surrender love that can take a knife to both your hearts.

I wonder which Tru and Veronica had.

Perhaps theirs is bonus love – animal love.

I call it bonus because it hasn't a category – where you just shed analytical ambitions and ~~fuck~~ right there on your square on this earth in the dirt – never expected, just done.

Is bonus the truest love?

I'm back to basics, numbering something that can't be numbered.

Interesting woman has been traveling with me since grade one, appearing and reappearing in different forms ever since.

I confess my fantasy of Interesting Woman to Arnold, he laughs out loud. Arnold sends a certainty I've neglected: 'When you are at camp, a woman you wouldn't normally pay attention to in town you'll pay attention at camp. Being at camp is like being drunk. The woman is beautiful until you wake up with her in town.'

This evening I catch Arnold sweeping the hall in front of our doorways at camp.

I ask him what he's doing, camp staff will clean the hallways.

'I know the staff clean the hallways but sometimes in the evenings I notice a bit of dried mud from workers. In the morning I like to see a polished clean floor – it starts my day off right. If I see any liter in front of my or your room I pick it up, that way we start the day off right.'

That is the best thing I've heard – most will just wait for staff to clean up.

Arnold adds, 'Cleaners do their job better if we help them keep the area clean.'

'Sure, a higher standard, one sliver of dirt will be monstrous.'

'Absolutely.'

It is an idea I have been considering for the last year, though never made a concerted effort to change the stream.

My last job I cursed someone who was purposely-spilling coffee, pop, or juice in front of my door. I cursed Spirits when mud was left near my door. I began to equate it to an unlucky year, nothing I could do – scorned by Spirits. Secondly, I noticed the poorly kept road in front of our property in Cambodia, wondering if Spirit was following, warning.

Maybe my rationalization is not off – a change to the entrance of my living quarters can relate to my life. This project has gone very well; my doorway seems predominately at peace.

Thank you, Arnold, we are the perfect team, we look after each other, we work hard. Success at the job starts with hard work, hard work and relationships gives a man independence. A Safety Advisor can chase relief all day by laziness or he can work hard and create wellbeing.

We go to work early, set ourselves up before first coffee with the info we need, all the paperwork done. If an incident comes later we are ahead of the game. If no incident occurs we go farther ahead preparing for the next three days, always staying atop. This is confidence we have done more than our share of work, the job becomes easy, time is our time. We are free because we rule, we don't chase.

If you assist in a relationship and not thwart the relationship, the relationship can flourish.

I'm here because I'm required to be here, not because I'm needed... remember that.

Improve the experience – the best we can be.

Arnold offers to go into partnership with me as Safety Contractors but I have no intention of putting stress and energy in this pursuit. He'll say I'm doing it already for less pay – maybe I am, but inside my mind I'm not; I'm still a poet, not a Safety Advisor. I could make more money with schooling, training, buy a truck, go into business with him. I would be established – a pillar in the system, a label. Nothing wrong with it, a true strong man or woman can do it, the fake and weak cannot. I know what I am. I am not a pillar of society. I am not weak. I am not fake. I'm not part of the establishment. If I became a pillar of society, a cog in the establishment, I'd be the weak because I'd be fake.

Arnold will be triumphant because he wants to be – this is a place he has decided will bring him green grass, prestige – an established man capturing comfort.

I look for internal comfort.

You can't become what you are not – it will work for a while, a time being, and then it will end.

Again, what about money?

What about money? The human lie machine asks.

Fight, struggle, don't lose your soul.

As good as work sounds, as good as my job goes, I know I'm losing, I'm losing my skill.

It is my last day of work. I have my money, six weeks' pay. My author friend takes a photo of us together – history for now – he too has offered to go into business – investments, he'll teach me the way.

Interesting Woman I don't know, spiritual journey together, who knows. 'Now will you run home to your wife and kids?' she says as we hold both hands in the air, knowing the next move will be wrapping her arms around my neck and pulling us together, except we can't as her co-workers look in.

Yeah maybe this woman has something enjoyable but...

I haven't regret writing Screws.

Serenity is the solution – chemistry, camaraderie.

A portrait – you have to portray. The better the illusionist, the better the player.

I haven't had a spirited drink in over a month. I haven't slept well in a month, I've worked thirty-five days straight, thirteen hours a day... wonderful. The health of soberness is erased by lack of life – money for life is the trade.

My wife will say shut up; a person in Cambodia would kill to have this chance.

I decided the first day I started the job eight years ago to build barriers to what I don't want.

Poetry shouldn't have rules, make complete sense, be duplicated, mapped, or measured.

Simple, immediate, worst, unacceptable, can't – don't – mold, becomes poetry too.

—

Live in a Tree – Hide in a Cave

How did I forget Friedrich Nietzsche?

If I'm to write the influence of Nietzsche then I must write ten other influences and then fifty on top of them.

I wanted to write as a saint and yet I wrote un-saintly.

Do the un-saintly write as saints?

I wrote stories first and thought them silly unreal fantasies – then I wrote real stories I'd lived and I thought that's not interesting?

Next, I combined the real and unreal – I wrote my thoughts, it goes like that. I wanted to write about changing the world and then I wanted entertainment, sex, drugs, murder – there is no end. We live our life, we want fun, we want experience, we want money – we want to live saintly and un-saintly, we can't do all at once, or can we?

Absolutes.

Happiness is never complete.

Can you tell me there is a proper way to live?

A right way to die?

A single faith to believe?

Sound off!

So, write, yell, complain, deliberate, celebrate.

Laugh, hide, seek, destroy, create.

I'm supposed to say cry, I see it all the time.

Absolute Inconclusive.

Life.

Can one answer a question of many?

I need a thousand more words.

Five more trips, unlimited adventure.

There we go, wants!

My next story will be about desire – desire shall be lifted – tears – living is life – that is all – no promise, be satisfied in the breath of air.

Call it harmony, call it peace, call it higher level, call it as you like, Nirvana, now I can live with-out ~~fuck~~ – I have no ~~fuck,~~ I live with no ~~fuck,~~ yet I think I can't live without ~~fuck,~~ this is scorn of desire.

I can live without material, I can live without money. I have no desire for wealth, I want only essential money – you can have no essential money without having money and wealth itself.

Loop.

Paradox.

Alter the circle.

Free desire.

Go touch this sensation.

No answers, only questions, until you cease to wonder and be.

Have I found it, have I found this sensation?

Living, breathing.

Clear of desire.

I disagree.

My desire brings everything, brings a level of humanity that I haven't read, haven't heard – a level of thought, a level of travel, a level of outer and inner world one would think is only a dream, and without desire I can only wish it, with desire I can attain it.

Buddha, I love your ideas but I need to expand on some – 2,500 years ago was 2,500 years ago – humanity needed to be tamed and it needs to be tamed again. Advanced technic.

In the past, the human was skilled in Spirits, now the human has no Spirit, they have machines.

The Venezuelan Panther and a few others gave me flight from inner to outer – through desire.

I'm spoiled – not by my family, by myself. For years I'd lived with dregs and suffered to have the pain, the insight, to write, to transform self to a higher level – not the seen, the unseen invisible world. If I cannot voluntarily suffer, be ridiculed, wade in the waters of trouble, live undesirable, how can I attain the highest desirable?

Let your ears pop.

Take me high – high that I haven't felt since the Venezuelan lover, the Cambodian wife.

Neha, she gave me glimpse – practice, schedule, and mindset – of how important desire is.

Don't be a fool bingeing, devouring desire; if you bath in desire you may never leave and desire becomes burden, pain, and unattainable desire will begin again.

Take your hit, enjoy it, walk away unless decided you've had all you craved, can stay, breathe, exist in pleasure, soothing, haunting, claim desire – you are at peace, you are at wonder of experience, not wonder of want.

Go superstar.

Extreme fright brings detachment from self – a higher level of breath. Leave the body, levitate, astral plane, super powered, blessed, clever animal, how you attain, float in atmosphere beyond atmosphere, can have many streams – don't live without taking one even if you must exercise yourself to the edge of breath.

Desire.

A saint in one ear, a devil in the other – now we don't spend most of our time in imagination.

Imagination is created for us on technical machines.

So now I follow tradition instead of questioning an unknown – I question the machine.

At the same time, I'm in touch with the invisible world, the spiritual world, what-ever it is – I haven't decided which is real, which is moral = machine or invisible spirit. In Cambodia they are more in touch with spirits, ghosts. I must say machines tend to tell us truths to entertain right or wrong. The human may one day be part machine. I can't say half-machine or a little bit machine because what the human consist of is still a question – we keep finding what used to be invisible parts.

I'd say the brain is a machine wrapped in protein, and the mind – the mind is the unknown, forever with thought.

The mind, the spirit, not part of the body

The Brain, human – a machine hidden deep in muscle.

Will we find a microscopic chip in the brain?

The mind, our savior, our true self, our true thoughts – the brain runs our body, our mind runs our invisible spirit. Well, I have terrible information for you.

The mind is the machine and the brain is the human.

The brain is you, the human and the mind is the machine.

The mind receives invisible signals from a machine that you can't see – running you left, right, everything that you thought to do, a signal to your mind sends you opposite views, pleasurable views – the controller is the mind.

The mind signaled by a machine should worry us.

Brain is spiritual you from the inside shone through the outside – the outside invisible world is how we receive wireless invisible insane and sane unstoppable info.

Does the mind tame us – or unleash us?

Shut the mind off you say and just use the brain – give me the switch.

The machine, the master, has diseased the brain, your most valuable tool with drugs – with disease – you rely mostly on the mind, fueled with information through machines instead of creating the world that your brain has stored for thousands even millions of years, all that information distorted by a mind, a disruptive machine questioning without answers because a machine is just a machine and the human is living, growing, dying bleeding, breathing, creating, and seeking.

Yes, we built the mind.

Did we build the Spirits? Is this the highest level of existence?

Just like a book influencing you – the invisible mind that intrigues the brain.

The invisible mind speaks through the brain.

It never stops, all the information in the brain, good, bad, ugly, honest, crooked, delightful.

Addictive – so addictive we don't even know the mind is separate.... we're humans hooked.

Dream commercial over. Now back to the story.

All I thought to do today changed as I wrote.

I was to write about conquering desire. I was to write about creating a story. I was to write about why I say machine talks to me from inside my brain and my only relief is my spiritual mind. Now all the pages I've written have turned upside down – this is writing. This is creating. You lose your-self. The invisible world takes your sentences, explores theories, argues ideas – this is free, this is freedom. A story board can't be kept, an outline must be refused because when unworldly grabs hold of you, finds tunnels and sights, to beauty, to terror, to insightful unexpected rewards, you went for a purposeful walk to the store, and ended up at a park or a bar not near the store.

When you learn to write you learn to speak – you already have the stories down complete.

I realize today that desire – accepting, admitting, realizing, is the next level.

———

12

HAVE A DRINK NIBBLES the ear, plays the hurt, challenges good health – good mental health. A drink will set me straight, a drink will shape good health. Terrible fight – wicked inner spell – religion becomes powerful for a drunk; reading, reflecting, searching those good books. Self-help, read them all in a few days. I write sober, read *Siddhartha* by Hermann Hess. Tru would be drinking beer, Veronica not much; a glass of wine, a flavored spirit.

Visiting my family, liquor in many ways is available.

I hibernate.

It has been four days since I left camp. The airport to Cambodia looms.

My Ruins finished, I can come and go to Lake Wapa.

Beat, Burnt, OD'd, and it was all done in his neighborhood that was thought impenetrable. He died in his home.

The authorities are not ruling out foul play.

Maybe it was OD first?

I wonder what happened to his dog?

Rumors, mumblings, say it was a targeted killing close to home – sometimes the top dog is run off by the pack. I guess it wasn't Veronica that killed him – I can say a woman could never have a comfortable life with Tru. As much as I liked Tru, he can't be considered a family man.

Some say he was a police informer. I laugh; they are all police informers or government tipsters, they all cheat and when they are caught they seek revenge, when they don't like a competitor it's easier to call the government or police than run them out of town. 'Men of respect' is the biggest con yet.

Maybe Veronica knew the hit was coming and split. Maybe their relationship wasn't a secret... security and criminality bad for business. Tru's name stretches far and wide in Lake Wapa and so does Veronica's. The security business mixed with the shady dealings of Tru is intriguing. Perhaps I was the fool, perhaps they've known each other for years, perhaps they have been in business together.

As far as I know I'm wrong about them being in a relationship before I introduced them, but the business end of it, the security and criminal business is an interesting twist. Perhaps, just perhaps, they were involved in more than sex – perhaps money was at the end of the stick.

There has to be a reason Veronica left. She is not dead – vanished, though the police say she is not a missing person, just a person no longer in Lake Wapa.

For many days I think Veronica is the smartest woman, an advanced being, a future human – she never pushed, she taught me, helped me, let me go away and live, perhaps she foresaw this Tru tragedy, and found the ideal solution.

Who finished Tru's ways? I don't know.

Why did Veronica run from Lake Wapa? I don't know.

Neha has gone to India with her husband and children.

As part of my debt proposal agreement I must receive debt counseling.

My debt counselor is gentle. I politely listen, he understands after ten minutes that I'm ahead of the game, that I've extorted the bank.

Am I better off? The only people better off are the ones doing something with a purpose, a goal that they love accomplishing, a struggle.

Take care of your family, secure your family, and yet you have to make yourself happy, otherwise an unhappy family will slip to the damned depths.

'It must be hard being away from your children?' my debt counselor asks me.

'It is harder raising children in debt than being away,' I say.

I look at my time away from my children as the Odyssey, a great test of life. They survive and if they don't – wasn't to be. I don't video call my family much as it makes the pain worse and the high when I see them in person lower. Intense lows and weaker highs is technology, it is bad enough I can call four times a week or three times a day.

Technology can take your imagination in a crazy direction – or you can trust technology, it can give you a false sense of control and take your mind to deep despair, viewing half-truths on video screens.

With Technology, travel is no longer the adventure, technology is.

Life is never comfortable unless you have inner freedom. Only you can find it – comfort in life. Religion, spirituality, philosophy, science, technology, is only a vehicle to a wider world that you need to find yourself.

I remember the moment when I said yes to the idea of tackling the credit system – when I really said yes! When I pushed forward with the physical money, the first thirty thousand gone. And when I say gone, you have to believe the money is gone, otherwise the plan will not work. You have to believe you don't have the money otherwise you'll spend it, pay it back, chicken out, fail.

Naïve freedom. Naïve privacy.

I ran into a friend of Tru's, the woman who was to be married the first day I visited Tru at his home.

She looked well healthy – smiles and respectable – maybe it was a good thing she did what she did before she was to marry. She stepped out of her SUV, walked over, and asked me if I'd heard about Tru.

I had.

'Too bad,' she said. 'Tru was an interesting guy. Are you surprised?' she asked.

'No, not really. I was when I heard, but now, after some clear thought, I'm not surprised.'

'I know. Come here.'

She put her arms around me. 'It was very nice to speak with you.' She looked at me with compassion. 'I'm different now than ... well, you know, the last time you saw me.'

I understand.

As she walked away I asked,

'Do you know what happened to Tru's dog?'

'Dead. Somebody poisoned his dog a few weeks before they found him.'

I wanted to ask her what she knows, if she knows about Veronica.

I don't.

—

Honey - Home

A vulture picking at my clothing – yes, I want clothing on when I die – next to my flesh. Bones are left – scattered clothing, my sculptured snake ring – nobody stole it yet. Mark it – my last step.

I thought raising vultures to cure my death but now I want to live-forever or a mighty long time. Money problem and money problems can turn to health problems and health problems can lead to death, so I can forget about money because I have all life to figure them out – so health problems disappear. Year zero has way past begun. I wanted to die, that was the cure, and now the cure is to live.

When my wife told me not to go down that road as I held myself down – I was prepared, I'd already been lost in South America, lost in North America. I listened to her – I didn't walk down that road in Cambodia, I threw my bag of experiment away.

Have children and I'll understand Cambodia, I thought, and still I wonder.

I've read when the human liver is consumed; it turns the whites of eyes yellow.

My wife has a yellow tinge in the what-would be the white of her eyes.

I asked her if the yellow in the whites of her eyes is from eating human liver.

Hesitantly, she answered, 'Maybe.'

I like to think she has eaten human liver so I can understand, understand her beautiful, curiously, flawed eyes.

I eat squid, I eat cow, I eat pig, I eat frog, I eat insect, I eat shellfish, I eat game, I eat everything that someone somewhere says not to eat. What am I? The anti-religion, the vegan devil, the anti-environmentalist, the non-believer, will I suffer when all the common believers bask in glory when they die to live and I'm dead? How does it matter when I'm dead?

Will I suffer for what I ate?

Instead should I abstain, live weak, go hungry, and then be rewarded with the cleanest death, the warmest death?

Do what you like – eat – die.

My wife interrupts my thoughts. She's so clever scolding me about my dreams. I scream her name to come near and she blasts me with,

'Where have you been today?'. My wife laughs. 'Out there traveling the sky or with a sexy Chinese girl? No – not Chinese, maybe Soviet?'

She's right I've been away today – I didn't make it to Chinese or Soviet or space.

I'd met a Vladivostok girl that I've never told my wife about just in case I'd like to travel up to the former Soviet Union sometime.

My wife still likes to say Soviet. I can see my wife as a child in the 1970s.

She'd wake up not to the school bell but the Regime's bell educated not in school but Year Zero philosophy of the Regime. Work, learn nothing of any outside world, eat little. Learn what in principle seemed like a bright start, the world started over from scratch, no past, no future, no religion, no money, a world not similar to the others of this earth.

No shoes to wear.

And me, what was I doing? I was waterskiing in the summer, hockey and snow skiing in the winter, my first school dance in 1979.

I'm jealous of her life and she's jealous of mine.

My wife is gracious. We asked for the same, a rocking chair and children for the sake of not when we're young, but an investment for when we're old.

In the morning my prick has a blister as big as my thumb. I say, 'Doctor.'

My wife speaks, 'Let me see.'

'No doctor,' she says. 'Ant bite you... wait two days. The ant bite you because you are not a friend.'

Apparently, an ant has bit my prick because I'm not a friend of the insect, I'm a foreigner in her country.

My wife thinks she's a friend of the insect because her ancestors are buried in the ground and mine are not.

She'd like me to believe that she can summon insects in retaliation of my wondering thoughts. Nope, I've seen through her performance.

If I can't live with the insect, what kind of man am I?

My body is a friend to the insect, that's why the insect comes – the insect doesn't like her, that's why it stays away. Slowly I have less and less insect bites, I have developed a defense – I'm not so much of a friend, soon I'll be an enemy, I've conquered her blood, the land, the animal, the reptile, and next the insect.

My wife spoke sure, my cock surrendered and the swelling subsided.

Touché, my love.

I'd told a police man to frig off – simple words, 'You frig off.' The next night I went to sleep with a slight notion the policeman may offer some thugs to visit my property late in the evening, torch my place.

Our dogs started barking insanely – the threat has come.

Here we go, there's going to be a fight.

I go to the kitchen and see the door is open – my daughter is outside, she yells, 'Snake . . . Cobra!'

I'm happy; a cobra snake, dancing, spiting at each of three dogs surrounding it.

This is a sure sign I'm lucky this time.

No threat, the cobra came instead.

The messenger.

My wife says kill it – kill it now, you want a snake or you want your children safe? Think about it.

I have thought about it – the snake is my protector.

Human, nature, animal, reptile, insect, and bacteria entwined.

I didn't kill the messenger.

My daughter captured the snake for the evening and in the morning. I called someone to pick up the cobra and release it in the jungle.

Yeah, I know the cobra was rather small.

Nevertheless. A danger averted.

Which reminds me, I was stung by a scorpion – my first time. Felt like broken glass being injected by a large syringe into my back and then spreading inside like a water balloon.

When we saw the scorpion fall from my shirt to the ground, my son says to me, 'That's just a small scorpion, they only hurt a little bit.'

'Great.' I said.

I'd never been stung by a bee until I was in my early twenties. I was mad . . . many were experienced in this sensation, so when I saw a bee on the ground I slipped off my shoe and stepped deliberately on the bee with my bare foot. I was stung, no allergic reaction. Good.

This was a time when I didn't understand that killing without reason would be a hinder. Well, fortunately, I had selfish reason. I don't know what pay back came of this event but yes, I was in a funk for some years and yes, this one event can't be the sole reason.

I'll take the bee over a jellyfish any day.

Paralyzed by an electric whip – is the touch of the jellyfish.

I stop writing with the sound of my wife's voice.

'You want tea, Honey?'

Yes, please.

13

———

THE FRUIT TREES HAVE grown – lotus bloomed.

I was blinded by a light, a light with stars the kind you see before you pass out, the kind I saw in Peru with shaman, the kind I saw on the hospital bed – the kind I see in extreme fright, the kind I saw when I made a decision to challenge the banks.

This time the black with shining stars is the climax of making love with my wife – the full circle has been accomplished, the rest is just the physical steps.

Coffee is beating tea – I am beating Spirited Drink, no longer crave to lose my mind, more a fear of losing my mind.

This is a story of being away.

Good aura wherever you've been, hauntings aren't distinct have neither borders nor time.

Jetlag is over.

I've learned that I may be a machine = I ignored it for a number of years. Today I admit, it is a truth that has to be admitted, if I'm to learn my mistakes.

We make the same mistakes over and over again annoyingly. The only conceivable answer is we are machine.

When you look under a microscope at the two-legged creatures making deliverers on our cells, it is evident we are some kind of machine – as they have their job, we have a job in this universe. It has nothing to do with earth; earth depends on the sun. Destroy earth and move on, how does that sound? As damaging as hearing we are mere machines. Each of us has our place, no matter how hard you try to do or be something else. Think it, write it – even the greatest genius has their weakness, forget perfect, perfect is all around us, perfect is the mechanism to build you the imperfect.

The imperfect trip to perfection is the perfect trip

To run your machine, you must understand the machine, what a machine is capable of, what adjustments are needed, if you need to turn the volume down. If you let the machine run unattended it will run into a brick wall.

Still, you will never believe you are a machine until you make yourself and still you won't believe it until you step inside yourself. 'A Machine' that you yourself built and still you won't believe it.

Wait – stay alive is most important, to see future is past.

Machine asks, 'If you are a machine then who made you? A machine can't make it-self.'

A micro system builds an organic machine. A micro system builds with material it generates just as we use raw material created to build machines – the micro uses created grown material to harness us.

Machine says, 'You are human, you create, you build the machines.'

If we the human can build a machine than why can't a million organisms working together build a machine?

'The animal and insect doesn't build machines.'

Different abilities, different concepts.

I've always found machines unimpressive – does this mean I'm closer to the animal?

'Answer your own question.'

Toady's machines are unimpressive because they are ancient. Humans are impressive, not machines.

'I thought you said human is a machine?'

Exactly.

Full circle.

Cut and paste; take a bunch of poems, combine them to a story. Take a skill combine them to an art. Take a bunch of organisms, combine them, and you have human.

Cut and paste wasn't revolutionary, it was elementary.

Punk rock.

—

After months, thousands of kilometers away from my wife, I was uncertain in marriage.

I bought the novel *Adultery* by Paulo Coelho for the long flight home. You could say I chose the book, it didn't choose me. But that isn't at all what happened – I choose the author.

In the *Adultery,* a sexy well-to-do married woman tells of her desires outside of raising two children and loving her husband. Her confessions penetrate mine and I suppose everyone else's marriage – a fear we all have and yet it is a fear you are thankful to understand when reading the story; nothing is perfect, nothing will ever be perfect. If you are at the top = knocked over, at the bottom = pushed down, and if you are in the middle = you have only yourself to find trouble.

I needn't have worried.

My wife and I danced like we did years before.

I wouldn't say we are comfortable but we have comfort in our marriage.

The story *Adultery* prepared me for the worst and I accepted it.

If I hadn't prepared, maybe my temper, maybe hers, jealousy, family, weakness, maybe a smile at another woman, a brush on her by a man could have set our sail adrift.

The worst I'd accept – therefore nothing except disaster could spare me from love.

Learn what you must accept in a relationship and when the truth is revealed, you've already been healed so you can move on or accept it.

—

I walk to my entry gates and clean – let the tunnel breathe smooth.

If I'm to believe in nature, my wife's place looks good. Though not perfect I can see I still have much work to do.

Before in front of my house the path unbalanced, untidy, un-kept – I was neglecting.

My wife says she'll give me two women next time we go to the city – a present for washing, freeing the land.

If your entrance is un-kept it extends through all aspects of life, as this is the first impression, a sign of your whole life.

You do not need gold at your gates; you will have thieves. You may have a crumbling gate just free it of debris – polite, fearful, whatever you like – maintain.

Art and theatrics come in many forms. Some like the illusion of a derelict place but behind the scene it is exquisite.

What you prefer – pride. Free of unwanted – your universe is clear to learn, expand.

Be aware of the melted tree, the shouldering plant - it is coming for you, the rain if you need sun, and the torturous sun when you need sprinkling rain. You cannot change the year, or the weather, you can only adapt, acclimatize, take care of what you have.

At first it may be a struggle tidying your entrance until, one day, others will help clean your path. Don't become a burden, don't depend on them, soon enemies, friends, spirits, ghost, animals, will avoid to poison your way.

The task of a respectable path will become easy, enlightening, fun. Though you are one with the world you are not one inside, you are many, as many as in the world you see.

I don't know which one starts first, the Ruins, the Lotus, or the Dynamic, if I die first, or am I born first, or is it all instantaneous?

It is near impossible to write something – easy to think about, plan it, but to work it . . . ~~fucking~~ impossible. Go ahead and sit, I say to the story.

My daughter is at the door – she's smiling beautifully – now giggling, as she can't get the words out. She's in-between sixteen to seventeen years of age.

She continues to smile as she tells me a story.

My daughter invited her friends to sleep in the shelter, three girls, two boys, plus my daughter. Last night one of the boys went outside to take a piss.

First mistake, I said, why go outside when there is a toilet in the shelter?

My daughter laughs, 'Yes, I don't know why he went outside. Maybe he was drawn outside by something.'

She tells me the rest of the story.

While he was taking a piss, a ghost appeared.

Petrified, shaking like mad, he ran back into the shelter to be consoled as he'd began to form tears. His friends held and settled him down, believing his ghost sighting to be true with my daughter confirming, 'Yes, we sometimes have a ghost on our property.'

My daughter tells me, 'I don't know if we can sleep in the shelter tonight because my friends are scared. I told my friends don't be scared, we'll leave the light on, and not to go outside.'

Enter my wife. She laughs. 'Tonight I will really give them a scare. A lesson to your friends on this property. . . behave or be haunted.'

They slept on the porch of the main house instead.

Sometimes I think my wife constructs the ghost episodes herself. She likes the idea of a haunted property.

I can't give her all the credit. My mind has to take some too.

I've begun to embrace the hauntings, a haunted property with a ghost is maybe the best security.

In fact, I have started to present my own ghosts.

There is no end to the ghost story, it will always be near, it is a matter of subduing it, keeping it happy and it will haunt for you.

—

I have passed the urge. I have settled; it isn't for my daughter, my son, or because I was locked up in camp, it is me; I have no care for drunk or drink.

It is how I feel now, how I feel today. When you hear from me again, it may change.

South East Asia is not what you expect – a place of paradise is myth. A place to run, to hide, is all it is.

I love it.

Sunbathing for the first time in years – I was never relaxed enough to lay in the yard and sun, now I'm sunbathing every few days.

My youngest daughter, loud: 'Let's go swimming, Dad.'

—

Alarms ring fast; it has only been four weeks but work has sent me a message for a job – I'm going back to work.

The tunnel of hell is gone – maybe I over-reacted it seems now – life isn't a ticket handed to an event that already has good reviews. Humanity has a thought – some sway bright, many despair.

Most times in life you never do know what happened, what really happened. I could write it out for you, tell you what happened.

I don't want to.

Real is vague, fleeting.

The money I made from the bank is nothing – it is material, it is investment, in my pocket I'm not wealthier.

14

SHOCK THE MEAT AND the being, the soul, will wake up. All they have to do is grow the meat, attach it to the stream and you will have human feelings – ~~fuck~~ we are there now. However, it will never have mind. The mind is the joker, the unstable, the unsettling, the devil, the genius, and the, I don't know why they've done this – when you can't explain something, it is the mind. The machine can always be torn apart and explained.

We are living backwards, traveling to the beginning. The beginning has long past, yes?

When we have finished here on Earth we'll have built the beginning and live the past.

Machine says, 'You're disturbed.'

Lake Wapa is warming up – blue water, green trees.

When I once hated work, I now like it – I could never dream I'd be looking forward to work.

Split it – bust up life – so you can live it.

Take a chore you are uncertain you can complete.

I'm understanding karma, I'm understanding cause and effect. I'm understanding the laws of nature. I'm the clean angel.

The bender for a day is over, family man. Working man.

My mother picks me up at the airport. I have a few days with her before I fly to work.

I expected to call Interesting Woman – I hoped to see Neha – this is what I thought.

What I thought, what one thinks is really the same as a dream or a bet you think you'll win.

What I see is a message on my phone from Veronica.

She's not dead. That's good.

Veronica will pick me up for lunch. No chance for escape it is a one and a half-hour drive up to the mountain resort for lunch near the home she's staying.

She starts the conversation, 'Neha says hi. She quit working for the new company, you know what she is doing now?'

'I don't know.'

'Working for the competition. Yeah, she quit when she went to India. I didn't know you'd be in town. I thought you'd be working or in Cambodia.'

My mind abounds with what happened between her and Tru. I'm not listening to her chatter except the parts about Neha.

I wasn't so surprised Veronica disappeared. I'm surprised she reappeared.

Veronica can be emotional, rash resolutions – she locks in, tries not to change her mind.

Veronica gave up on a child after her divorce. She would only date a man that was not from Lake Wapa, though sleep with a man from Lake Wapa, or she'd date men from Lake Wapa and not sleep with them – she'd sleep with men from out of town or on vacation. She's tried all different scenarios, combinations, and none have overwhelmed.

A large multinational security company had an offer on the table for Veronica's company for months and she put her homes up for sale with a guarantee to the multinational that if her homes sold, she'd sell.

She had three months to make the sale. It only took two months. The multinational bought her home at the resort.

Veronica traveled to Central America, searching for a guesthouse she can lease – if she likes the work, she'll try this guesthouse business for a time.

Marry, adopt children, build a business is her plan.

'Everyone tells me to start a security business in Central America – I laugh – I'm running away,' Veronica quotes.

It is easy to run away. Staying away is the problem.

It isn't the dream you must satisfy, the dream is to keep you striving, a dream cannot make you happy, you must be happy already and live a dream.

That leaves me with the question – what is with you and Tru?

She brings it up. 'Did you hear about your friend Tru?'

'I have I did.'

'There are so many stories going around.'

'Someone told me they heard it was a professional hit because Tru was a police informant,' I fish.

'L Ce, I talk to the police, I don't hide this, this is my business. I've worked with the police with information on Tru in the past. I know all about his dealings. Tru wasn't a police informant. He talked to the police, he treated the police like a regular citizen. The police knew what he was about but they left him alone. Although, just because you don't touch it with your hands doesn't mean you aren't involved. The laws are not always right but you shouldn't invest in harmful things.'

'Like Coca-Cola, insurance, and the banks?'

'Come on. Sometimes I must do security for a man who beats his wife or cheats his business partners too.'

'Like Tru, sometimes he must do business with unworthy people. He must have closed his eyes, but inside he knew when a kid dies in this town maybe he profited from it. And in the end that same thing came back and killed him.'

'When you say it like that, it doesn't sound good.'

'And still you bought a bicycle from him.'

'I did.'

'Some of the things Tru did might have been illegal but not wrong, and others legal, though truly hurtful.'

'This world has the written and the unwritten rules.'

'Correct. That is why we have religion, another law, another judge.'

'I don't need religion to know what is right and wrong.'

'Is that what you think? Where did you learn that?'

'Something I know.'

'You learned from religion when you were a little boy.'

'Okay Veronica.' I smirk.

'You just don't remember – you learned through your parents, learned in school, and most through religion.'

'Before religion people just did whatever they liked without consciousness of good and bad, right and wrong?'

'Yes, correct.'

'Veronica...' I say her name with a slow long expression like she's lost her mind.

'Tru should have went to church. Look how good you are now after going to church with me – you have a family, a loving wife, a steady job, a home, good morals, living a fulfilling live.'

'Veronica, you think all this is because of my time in church with you?'

'Yes, you quit drinking when you went to church with me, correct?'

'Yes, but it isn't related, I decided to quit drinking and then went to church.'

'Is that what you think? God would think differently.'

'Sure.'

'You might not realize it but that was the beginning of the change of your life. God directed you.'

'Wholly fuck, Veronica! Stop it!'

'Stop what...the truth?'

'The truth is I went to church so I could ~~fuck~~ with you whenever I liked!'

'Doesn't matter the excuse, because it worked.'

'It didn't work, I couldn't ~~fuck~~ you whenever I liked.'

'Because silly, you didn't want to. You've become a wonderful person.'

'Okay,' I start to laugh – she is playing, trying to ~~fuck me~~ right now as she moves close, petting me with her glowing eyes. Stay away Veronica, I know what you are up to.

I turn away.

'L Ce,' she says softly in a sweet voice.

I turn, engage her eyes for a minute, before saying let's go eat, I'm hungry.

Maybe she did kill Tru.

—

At lunch Veronica asks, 'Do you know a guy named Gragon? He lived at the end the road where Tru lived. The police questioned him.'

'Yeah, they sometimes call him Dragon. He was there when Tru and that guy were fighting with the pipe and machete – he was the short guy, brown shoulder-length hair, a little older than I am.'

'I don't remember him.'

'Why would you? Do you think he had something to do with Tru's murder?'

'If he was murdered.'

You don't think he was killed off?

'The courts will decide what we should know.'

'What do you think Veronica?'

'This Gragon hasn't been charged that I know of. He admitted to being at Tru's the night he died. They are still calling it foul play – overdose by design. Ongoing investigation – Gragon moved away from town, closed his business.'

'You know a lot.'

'Tru bought a security camera from my company, we installed it for him.'

'Really.'

'Yes. His dog was poisoned. A week before his dog was poisoned, two young tough brothers came to Tru's backyard threating him because one of the brothers was seeing the same girl as Tru – or Tru was seeing his girlfriend.'

'The college girl.'

'Yes, her boyfriend had an alibi when the dog was poisoned; he was working out of town, but not his brother. He wasn't working when Tru died though. He's a suspect I'm sure – I don't know what their alibi is.'

'Together.'

'Ha, ha, ha, – guilty.'

'I don't know. All we are talking is things we don't know. Dreaming.'

'You aren't comfortable talking about it?'

'I don't know if I should be comfortable – I think about a lot of people who have died of why and how they passed. I think it never stops. Even if they were sick, I think of the lead ups, the things they did through life and what they could have changed.'

'We all do that – the leading factors – this is why you must live a clean life, a life that isn't filled with bravado and non-truths – live a life you're proud of. And when you die people won't think of what you could have done differently, they'll say wow that person lived a complete life. This can be said even if a person has died young.'

'No regrets.'

'In a way – it can't be defined – you have to watch that you don't say it a certain way as then it will seem a person passed because they deserved it, or were not living the right way, doing the right thing, making the correct choices. It isn't about dying, it is about living – so when you do die you're not fearful. You are proven, haven't left anything behind you needed to correct.'

'You could say Tru had nothing left to correct other than his entire life – he lived on luck for a long time. He seemed happy.'

'Tru died maybe how he wanted except with Gragon instead of a woman. He might have changed that part of it.'

'Maybe he loved Gragon, they were best friends for many years.'

'Die with the ones you love.'

I'd like that but many wouldn't.

Before I met my wife and children I wanted to die alone in the desert.

'How well did you know Tru, Veronica?'

———

Veronica's account as we sit parked in her car:

They collided like comets.

Veronica and Tru met on the sidewalk. 'You have a security company, don't ya? Somebody killed my dog yesterday,' is what Tru said to her.

And Veronica said, 'Hey, you still got that mountain bike for sale?'

Evening dinner was asking too much of Veronica.

Tru's talk of need for security intrigued Veronica and she agreed on drinking healthy shakes together.

Tru thinks the college girl's boyfriend may have been behind his poisoned dog.

You'd think a solution would be to stop seeing the college girl. But nope, the college girl and Tru have an arrangement and they hadn't stopped seeing each other.

College girl still saw her boyfriend when he was in town and Tru when her boyfriend was working out of town. Her cake and eat it too.

Veronica invited Tru over to her house to take a look at the used security camera equipment she had stored in her basement.

I was at work. Veronica knew I wouldn't be home.

They debated the best option for home security. Tru even pricing out how much it would cost to hire a patrol car to drive around his neighborhood a few times a night.

I mention to Veronica, why he didn't just pay a couple of his goons as lookouts?

She laughed and thought the same – she asked Tru the question.

Tru felt having friends as lookouts can cause more problems than are solved. While a security company just calls the police and professionally records information, friends find their own solutions.

Tru previously only had a dummy camera installed on the side of his house.

As Tru was to leave Veronica's, he pulled Veronica close to say goodbye and kissed her in the kitchen. An unexpected kiss, she kissed him back. Wow, that was a surprise – Neha was near, she could see and hear. No fear of more than kissing. Veronica could stop him. Business.

Neha asked Veronica what that was about in the kitchen.

Veronica told her she was going to buy a mountain bike from him.

'Not the mountain bike, the embrace and kissing on the lips?' said Neha.

'Sweetening the deal – don't worry nothing will happen. He's a friend of L Ce's.'

'I see,' smiled Neha.

'I'm going to pick up a mountain bike from him maybe in a few days whenever I drive out to see him. I might sell him some security cameras and sign him up.'

'Oh, maybe an expensive kiss for him?' Neha burst out laughing.

'Yes, if he doesn't take the camera's I want a discount on the bike.'

'Must be nice not to be married, you can make deals.'

'Funny, it would work better if I was married as you always have an excuse not to go all the way.'

'What about blackmail? What if he blackmailed your husband?' Neha's eyes were as wide as her smile.

Veronica returned comically serious, 'My husband would be in on it for the business.'

'This is why you are single.'

'I never thought I'd get along with a guy like him. L Ce can never find out, he'd laugh at me after I'd crucified his friend. I spoke badly about L Ce's friend – L Ce would never understand.'

That was Veronica and Neha as told by Veronica and played out in my mind.

Veronica leaves a gap and goes straight to the night before I viewed her in Tru's driveway.

'I went to his place, looked at the bike, agreed on it. He agreed on signing for a security camera to be installed by my company. I wished I could have said goodbye to you, L Ce. I was busy with the sale of my company and home. I missed you. Maybe I wasn't ready to say goodbye – I'm sorry.'

'I waited for you Veronica to say goodbye but you never came home – you were gone all night.'

'I slept at Tru's that night – nothing happened.'

Silence.

'Tru talked about his girlfriend troubles. I drank some wine and it began to snow. Really awful weather that night, you remember?'

Last snow-fall of the year.

'He offered me a bed in the extra room. I drank another glass of wine waiting for the snow to stop and soon I'd drank too much and slept on the spare bed. That is all. I never ever saw him again. My team went over, set up the security camera at his house a day later.'

Still silent.

'Tru didn't care about dating or having sex with me, though I'm sure he would have. He was using me I think – make friends with a security company.'

'Maybe.'

'Yes, I could tell by the way he talked, the question's he asked that he was trying to become secret agent partners. It intrigued me. I was curious of what he'd try and conspire. He was kind of a fun guy to be around.'

'I know.'

'He was really nice. If I didn't know what he was about – a girl could make a mistake with him. I was using him for entertainment and he was using me for some kind of scheme. Everything is about a deal with him. What he can get out of the relationship.'

That is true of everyone; people have different levels of what they need in a relationship.

'I knew I would see you again – we always see each other and talk.'

So, do you have the bike?

'Yes, he brought it to my office that morning. It's good. I'm taking it with me on my travels. Do you want to see it? I've been riding it.'

'Never.'

Veronica starts her rented car.

—

Before I leave to work, I have the chance to meet up with my niece and plant raspberry bushes – summer and autumn variety – in remembrance of my nephew, at my sister's place.

My nephew loved the raspberries my mother grew in her backyard.

I thought maybe seeing the future was my next step in the spiritual world but it is admittance.

I think it is admitting who you are, what you are to become, and who you have been.

Only then can you see the future.

Full circle hurry up or go slow... enjoy, glow, and grumble.

15

—————

The Case

WHEN SOMEONE PULLS a gun you are fearful, and then you become enraged – fear and then enrage – you talk, you settle the person down, make sense. Once the fear is gone, the enrage kicks in, you yourself become aggressive.

This is why they say if you are to pull a gun, pull the trigger.

A threat is retaliated by an action.

—

Tru, beat, burnt, OD'd. Dead, sitting at his kitchen table.

All true but not as badly as it sounded, except the death part. He wasn't beat dead, he wasn't burnt to the bone, a drug wasn't plunged into his skin.

Two blunt blows, one to the left side of his face and forehead, the other to the back of the head and neck area, with markings reminiscent of a butt end of a rifle. Burns to his left ear, hair, and right hand, from what appeared to be a butane torch – his blue sports jacket melted on the left arm; up to protect himself presumed. Blood rolled from his nose, a black eye.

The police found a few matching footprints on the trail, to a parking lot for access to walking trails in the forest at the base of the mountain near Tru's home.

Tru took this trail daily to sprint, walk, or jog, usually with his dog. Police think he went to meet someone after six pm. Phone calls, messages don't say anything. Tru can be seen on his security camera arriving, parking his car in the alley driveway and entering his house at six pm. Dark night already. He cannot be seen leaving – he could have left out of the front door. Footprints inconclusive, dry. A security camera at the back of the house but nothing in the front.

Tru's dog died in the back yard.

Maybe part of the violence happened in his house, although there is no proof. There is proof at the trail parking lot, pieces of burnt fabric from his sports jacket, and blood.

The ground was mainly dry with a few soft spots. The snow mostly melted a couple of weeks before.

Footprints from the trail lead back to the road behind Tru's home.

Case closed, not completely; how'd he die?

The security camera captured a man coming to Tru's back door. Wearing a cap, sunglasses, a bulky black jacket. The person knocked, walked in at 8:45 pm, leaving the same way at 11:25 pm. The person in the video is seen leaving and entering multiple times, wandering around the backyard, driveway, and alley, smoking a cigarette mostly – at one time lying down, hiding for twenty minutes against the garbage bin. Another time, kneeling at the edge of the garage, spying on the alley for ten minutes.

A few days after Tru's death the police go to Gragon's home that is on the opposite street of Tru's at the end of the row of homes – across this street are the lower mountain trails.

Tru and Gragon longtime friends since school – Gragon is crazy as Tru, different though; Gragon is lower profile yet more caught up in the criminal world.

Gragon was crushing methamphetamine recently, the cheap man's drug – he'd become toxic for months, threatening friends. Something was bothering Gragon.

Tru distanced himself from Gragon, afraid like everyone else.

Tru refused to loan him money.

Gragon fit the description of the man on the security camera. The man on camera came and went the opposite direction of Gragon's home, his footprints lost when the alley meets the street.

When the police arrived at Gragon's it was perfect timing; Gragon was on a methamphetamine high.

Witnesses sat on his chesterfield as Gragon told a bizarre story to the police.

Gragon told the police that Tru worked with a team of ninjas that hid in the forest. He went on about Tru's ninjas making trouble for everybody – the ninjas were providing false information to the police while stealing and lying from the public.

'If you want to know the truth about Tru, talk to the ninja's. Sometimes the ninjas come into my home while I sleep, they have keys for all the homes in this area. They have keys to your police station too,' told Gragon.

The police took Gragon in – once in police custody he began to tell a different story.

Gragon's story:

Nobody told or asked Gragon to visit Tru – it was just a feeling he had. He wanted to check in on Tru, make sure everything was okay. Neighborhood watch. Make sure nobody was doing more than poisoning a dog.

Gragon didn't like to walk the alley at night, too dark. He preferred the dim streetlights. Gragon walked on the street behind Tru's row of homes and then walked back down the alley as Tru's home is only three houses in from the corner of the street.

He wore sunglasses and a cap because he always wore a cap and sunglasses; it was a habit, even at night – ask anyone.

Tru wouldn't tell him what happened, how he got plunked and burned.

Tru was mixing opiates and methamphetamine – needing quick relief he heated opiate pills and crystal-meth and then inhaled them. Ease the pain – his back sore, his head aching, he found it difficult to move.

Tru told Gragon to go outside every fifteen minutes as a lookout for real or imagery foes – Tru wasn't in a mood to be questioned or argued, Gragon listened.

Nervous and alone outside is why Gragon hid behind the garage and garbage bin.

Gragon said he was offered but didn't smoke drugs with Tru – Tru stoning alone.

Tru vomited in a bucket because it was too painful to walk to the toilet.

Feeling uncomfortable, Gragon left Tru's home, walking the same way he came.

Tru died sometime within the hour Gragon was seen on the security camera leaving Tru's home.

Tru was found the next morning by his girlfriend at 7:40 am – the back door was unlocked.

She was at home studying with a girlfriend the evening before (her alibi). Her boyfriend and his brother drinking at their parent's place (her boyfriend's alibi).

Nobody on the street could miss the police presences in the morning and all through the day.

Gragon left his home for work at 7:50 am. Missing the police. He drove the opposite direction the police traveled down the highway.

He worked as a delivery driver – used automobile, farm equipment, industrial parts, what needed delivery in a pickup truck or trailer he delivered. Dope included I can't swear but a good cover one could presume.

His work this day consisted of sitting standby in his truck near the industrial park, drinking coffee till 9:40 am when he received his first call for a drop off and delivery. Another pickup at 12:20 pm, delivered two hours away from Lake Wapa at 3:00 pm. No more calls except a call about Tru's death. Gragon still out of town, parked his truck and mourned Tru's death. He didn't arrive home till 8:00 pm that evening.

Why hadn't Gragon contacted the police?

Gragon felt Tru was dead already and needn't questions for answers he didn't have. Besides, he was tired.

When Gragon was taken in for questioning he tested positive for drugs – including the type Tru died from, yet he said he didn't take any drugs that evening with Tru.

Gragon told he began taking drugs when he heard of Tru's death.

Gragon's body a toxic fume.

Story 1 on the street:

Gragon may have known about Tru's troubles that evening in the trail parking lot – he may have been there with him.

Gragon brought the drugs to Tru's.

Tru didn't keep drugs in his home, didn't smoke drugs that anyone was aware of for years.

Gragon offered Tru the drugs for pain, mixing opiate and methamphetamine, too much, too strong, killing Tru. Gragon fled the scene.

Story 2 on the street:

Gragon hit Tru in the head with the butt end of a rifle and held the gun on him – burned him with a torch, forcing him to smoke a deadly combination of opiate and meth until Tru OD'd. Gragon was finishing Tru off in a speed-induced grudge – money, or misinformed, as Gragon was on a losing streak; he himself had been ripped off, and his business partners recently had been busted by the police. Tru refused to help Gragon out with a loan.

Gragon could have had help from others, he may have let them through the front door. He could have planted the blood and pieces of the blue jacket fabric in the trail parking lot – the footprints could easily be replicated with Tru's running shoes. Or he was with Tru in the trail parking lot from the start.

No rifle found.

No butane torch.

Tru and Gragon remained friends on the same street for years, something can erupt from nothing or compound for years, innuendos, secrets, crosses, and misunderstandings – a long-time circle that came to an end.

Story 3 on the street:

Almost everything Gragon said to the police true. Others were responsible. Tru went to the park – beat up, burned, in pain he somehow got his hands on opiate and meth. Possible the people that assaulted him provided him with the dope that killed him, or maybe personal stash – perhaps delivered to his front door, perhaps received the drugs from any one of his friends in the neighborhood.

—

Perhaps a message – 'Burnt' for ripping someone off. 'OD' for drug dealing. 'Beaten' because he had it coming. 'Murdered' for payback.

Tru's neighbor a close friend, has a security camera that views Tru's property edge, the opposite side Gragon walked. Tru's – neighbor was gone out of town that weekend – none of the neighbors saw Tru that evening, none of the neighbors saw Gragon that evening.

A small amount of drugs that killed him were found on Tru's kitchen table, nothing more. No stash of cash or illegal weapons.

You can only sit so long – stagnate the same things over and over until pressure and then split.

Nobody saw Tru leave or enter his home after six pm. Nobody saw anyone enter or leave Tru's front entrance. Nobody saw Gragon walking down the street. No security camera's viewed suspicious activity in the neighborhood.

Gragon should have called 911 – guilty or not-guilty if he knew Tru OD'd. In Canada there is a law called the Good Samaritan Drug Overdose Act. Immunity from simple possession charges for those who call 911 in an overdose case.

Unless he didn't want Tru to live or as he said he was never there when Tru died.

Gragon spent a day and night in jail and then wasn't seen.

Tru may have left and entered through the front door as not to be seen on the security camera; maybe he was carrying something or with somebody that he didn't want known or someone else didn't want known.

A list of what happened goes on incomplete.

Unsolved.

His kingdom infested.

Some say College Girl was the culprit – her boyfriend, or the unknown.

Smoking opiates and meth at fifty-three years of age – no wonder Tru died.

I say it was Spirits.

The Ninjas like Gragon said.

End.

—

I relish my privacy in real life as I give much experience in the stories I tell. Les Cook

Don't miss out!

Visit the website below and you can sign up to receive emails whenever Les Cook publishes a new book. There's no charge and no obligation.

https://books2read.com/r/B-A-BFOI-MBGAB

Connecting independent readers to independent writers.

Also by Les Cook

Lit for Nothin

The Program Illusion

Tempting Fiction

About the Author

I relish my privacy in real life as I give much experience in the stories I tell. **Les Cook**

www.ingramcontent.com/pod-product-compliance
Lightning Source LLC
Chambersburg PA
CBHW050419260626
47156CB00003B/1073